ACTS OF
Salvation

Acts of Salvation

Salvation

ELEANOR ALDRICK

Acts of Salvation

Copyright © 2020 by Eleanor Aldrick

Cover Design: Sinfully Seductive Designs
Interior Formatting: Sinfully Seductive Designs
Copy Edit: Ellie | My Brother's Editor

All rights reserved. No part of this book may be reproduced or used in any manner without written permission of the copyright owner except for the use of quotations in a book review. For more information, address: **eleanoraldrick@gmail.com**

This is a work of fiction. Names, characters, businesses, places, events, locales, and incidents are either the products of the author's imagination or used in a fictitious manner. Any resemblance to actual persons, living or dead, or actual events is purely coincidental.

FIRST EDITION

ISBN: 978-1-7345272-2-3

10 9 8 7 6 5 4 3 2 1

For My Mother.

The woman who taught me the value of hard work. Just like Cassie's mom, she held us together, working three jobs just to make sure we made rent and had food on the table.

I will forever be grateful for you and the valuable lessons you taught me.

I love you.

"It's impossible,"
said pride.

"It's risky,"
said experience.

"It's pointless,"
said reason.

"Give it a try,"
said the heart.

-author unkown

LA DIFICIL – BAD BUNNY

BOSS BITCH – DOJA CAT

TKN – ROSALIA & TRAVIS SCOTT

CAMBIARE ADESSO – DARK POLO GANG

NO JUDGEMENT – NIALL HORAN

FOREVER (FEAT. POST MALONE & CLEVER) – JUSTIN BIEBER

NOBODY'S SUPPOSED TO BE HERE – DEBORAH COX

LAY YOUR HEAD ON ME (FEAT. MARCUS MUMFORD) - MAJOR LAZER

Prologue
Cassie, Age 15

The sobbing turns back into yelling and I prepare for yet another round of 'How could you…' My mother's go-to question during these spats.

It's always the same. Things never change.

They fight. Dad threatens to leave. Mom begs him to stay. He verbally degrades her. She yells, and then he finally leaves, only to return a couple of weeks later right into the open and waiting arms of my mother.

I shake my head, unable to understand why anyone would put themselves through this hell over and over again.

But this is their routine. This is *normal*.

The front door slams shut, the deafening sound echoing in our small one-bedroom home, signaling the end of another fight.

My father has left—*again*.

The yelling has stopped but the sound I hate keeps looping in my ears, over and over. I hear Mother open and shut the bathroom door, no doubt trying to keep us from hearing her cry. *Too late.*

Unable to stand it any longer, I get up from my bunk and make my way to the door. I'm about to step out of the bedroom when my sister whispers, "Don't, Cassie. Leave her."

"I can't just leave her out there, Aria." I open and shut the door behind me before she has the chance to say anything else.

Slowly making my way down the tiny hall, I hear my mother's muffled sobs become louder. My heart physically hurts at the sound of such a strong woman breaking down for a man who isn't worth it.

I'm standing outside the bathroom door, hesitating, wondering if my sister was right when it flings open.

"*Dios mio!*" Mother exclaims. "What are you doing out of bed?"

Her usually calm and joyous face is now red and splotchy, her eyes bloodshot and swollen. "Mama." My voice cracks, unable to hide the hurt. "Why do you put up with him? We don't need him."

"He's your father, Cassandra. Don't say things like that." Mother wraps an arm around my shoulder and guides me back to the tiny room I share with two of my sisters. "Come on. Let's get you back to bed."

We tiptoe our way down the hall and across the tiny bedroom, trying to make as little noise as possible, but it's pointless. Everyone

ACTS OF SALVATION

is up.

Aria speaks as soon as we reach my bed, "Mama, why do you let him do this to you? He isn't worth it."

My thoughts exactly.

"One day, *mija*, when you fall in love you'll understand," our mother coos, trying to temper my sister's anger.

I scoff. My body unable to hold back its response to that ridiculous answer.

"And since you're up, I need to tell you something." Our mother begins to pace between the two sets of bunks we share. "Your father is going away for a little while and I don't know when he'll be back."

I roll my eyes. Here we go again. I could practically recite this speech in my sleep.

"But just because he isn't here, it doesn't mean that he doesn't love you. You girls are his pride and joy. He'll be back for you, I know it…" Her voice trails off as if she isn't really sure if that's true anymore.

It is. Not the part about him loving us, but the part about him coming back. When his money runs out, he'll be back.

Money.

My stomach grumbles at the thought, reminding me I didn't eat much for dinner. Rice and beans. It's always rice and beans. We eat it so much I think I'm going to turn into rice and beans.

"*Tienes hambre*, Cassandra? If you're hungry, I can fix you something to eat," Mom whispers from across the room.

"No, I'm okay," I lie, knowing it'll be another damn plate of rice and beans. Besides, with Dad gone, we'll have to ration what little food we do have. Money is always tight, but when he

3

disappears, so does our money. Mom has never confirmed this but I suspect he clears us out every time he takes one of his *trips*.

"I'm getting a job." My words hang in the darkness of the room before they register.

"Cassandra Maria Martinez, you are not getting a job," my mother rushes out. "You're only fifteen. All you should be worried about is school."

"That's not what I'll be worrying about when the power gets cut or you're working your third shift in one day just to make sure we make rent." I fling the pillow I've been clutching at Aria. "And you should get one too, instead of spending all your time with Jacob. You're just going to get yourself knocked up like Carmen, and if that happens then you can wave bye-bye to your dreams of going to college."

"If I'm getting one, then so is Ceci." Aria tosses the pillow up to our sister's bunk. "Stop acting like you don't hear us. There's no way you're still sleeping."

We get nothing but silence in response. *Well shit. Is Ceci even here?*

As if coming to the same conclusion, my mother bolts to the top bunk and pulls back the covers. Yup. Ceci isn't even here. Instead, we have a bunch of blankets rolled up in the shape of a body.

At least she missed out on today's theatrics. Unfortunately for her, our mother doesn't share the same sentiment. She releases a string of curse words in Spanish before lowering herself onto my bed. "That girl is worse than Carmen. At least Carmen waited until she was eighteen to sneak around. Do either of you know where she is?"

"Of course not," Aria blurts out. "If I knew, I wouldn't have thrown the pillow up at her."

"And you?" Mom turns her head toward me, raising a brow in suspicion.

"Nope." I shake my head and suck in my lips. I don't know for sure but even if I did, I wouldn't say. I'm no snitch. Taking the distraction for what it is, a blessing, I quickly change the subject. Maybe this will keep Mom off my back about the job.

Letting out a yawn, I make a show of being tired. "I'm going to bed. Hopefully Ceci doesn't need bailing out tonight."

"Cassandra!" Mother gasps. "Don't say things like that."

"Fine, fine. I hope she doesn't get pregnant." I snicker as my mother makes the sign of the cross before kissing her thumb, no doubt sending up a silent prayer.

Prayer. They need a whole lot more than prayer.

The one good thing about being the youngest of five is the fact that I've learned from all of their mistakes, and believe me, there have been many.

A chill creeps up on me, making my teeth chatter. Rolling over on my side, I bring the warm covers up to my chin and vow to never fall into the trap of love. It makes you stupid and weak—a damn fool—*and I'm nobody's fool.*

Chapter One
REN MORETTI

*L*IFE. IS. GOOD.

I'm driving my 1952 Jaguar XK down I-75, top down, letting the wind cleanse away the day's work. It's about to hit midnight and I'm on my way to meet up with one of my boys, William. Poor schmuck needs the distraction since his entire world has turned to shit. And everyone knows that a night of drinking and pussy is the perfect fix for a world turned upside down.

I exit the highway and make my way into the heart of uptown. As the resident manwhore, William trusts my judgment with picking tonight's rendezvous point. It's the hottest bar in town, with the best drinks, and of course the best women. There's no doubt my boy will find someone to take his mind off of the current dumpster fire that's his life.

I roll up to the valet and already see multiple prospects for the night. Handing over the keys to my baby, I let the man know she's not his toy to play with.

He gets it, offering a nod. "We'll be sure to keep her up front Mr. Moretti."

"Good. You take care of her and I'll take care of you. *Comprendi*?" I tilt my head, waiting for his verbal confirmation.

"Yes, Mr. Moretti, your girl is safe with us."

Feeling enough assurance that she's in good hands, I step inside to find William. He's at the bar, head down, staring into a tumbler of amber liquid.

"Let's turn that frown upside down." I pat William on the back with one hand and wave over the bartender with the other. As soon as he's within earshot, I let him know of tonight's plans, "We'll be heading to the VIP area. Please transfer whatever drinks he's had onto my tab and let the waitress know we'll be at my usual table."

"You don't have to do that, Ren. I can pay for my own tab." William rolls his eyes and shakes his head. "I'm not financially bankrupt, just emotionally."

There's no doubt in my mind that he can cover his drinks for the night. Hell, we're some of the wealthiest bastards in Texas, and that's saying something considering we're home to one of the oil capitals of the world.

But that's beside the point. The point is that I don't want William focusing on anything other than good old-fashioned debauchery.

ACTS OF SALVATION

"Whatever, man. I said I'd take care of you tonight and that means you ain't thinking about a thing. All you have to do tonight is focus your sad little eyes on beautiful ladies and whiskey." Nudging his shoulder, I guide him toward the roped-off area of the bar. *My second home.*

As soon as we're seated, the waitress places a bottle of Jack and a carafe of water in front of us. "Thanks, Cindy. You mind getting a bottle of Macallan 18 for my friend here? Just put it on my tab."

"Of course, Ren." Cindy bats her lashes before disappearing back into the crowd.

"Could she be any more obvious with how she was ogling you?" William chuckles.

"I'm aware Cindy has a crush on me, but there's no way I'd act on it. I don't shit where I eat and I definitely don't do complicated. Banging a waitress where I come to relax is just asking for trouble." I pour myself a rocks glass of Jack and water, my signature drink, before continuing. "Besides, we aren't here for me. We're here for *you.*"

"I'm fine. Really." William tries to convince me but fails miserably. The dark circles under his eyes and that glazed over expression tell a different story.

"Right. That's why you keep spacing out on me, staring into your glass of scotch as if it holds all the—" A blond at the bar catches my attention, effectively breaking my train of thought. "Normally, I'd call dibs on the beauty at the bar but since you're in such a funk I'll begrudgingly let you take your chances first." I roll my eyes and shake my head. He's done it again. Snapping my fingers in his face, I attempt to break him out of his trance. "Earth to William. Where the hell did you go?"

9

He slowly blinks his eyes before turning to face me. "Yes, I'm here, asshole. Just have a lot on my mind."

"Mhmm. Well, like I was saying, there's a hot blond at the bar. I'm heading over if you don't call dibs."

"She's all yours. Not my type."

"Since when are blonds not your type?" I start walking toward the bar, not really waiting for an answer. Frankly, the more I look at this woman, the more I realize I would *not* have been okay with William calling dibs.

She's stunning. Absolutely fucking gorgeous. I honestly don't think I've seen such natural beauty in a very long time.

Don't get me wrong, she's by no means granola. Her blond hair is styled in a long angular cut that ends just above her full breasts—breasts that I bet would feel amazing in my hands—and you can tell that she spent time on her makeup. I'm no expert but whatever she did is perfect. It all works to enhance her beauty, not mask it as most women do. You can even see her freckles poking through. *Who knew freckles would be so damn sexy?*

"So, are you going to introduce yourself or are you just going to stand there and stare at me like some creeper." The blond raises an eyebrow as she takes a slow sip of her martini, piercing through my soul with her haunting hazel eyes.

My breath catches, leaving me without air. *Those eyes.* I feel as if I've stared at them before, but there's no way. I would've remembered her face, those curves...

Quickly trying to recover, I slide onto the barstool next to her before delivering one of my classic lines, "Did you know that Frank Sinatra's favorite drink was the dirty martini?"

"No, that was his favorite drink to serve guests. His favorite

ACTS OF SALVATION

drink was Jack and water." Her brows furrow as she looks at my drink. "But I have a feeling you already knew that."

"A girl who knows her Sinatra trivia. I think I might have to marry you."

What. The. Fuck. Did I just say that?

The blond coughs as she spits out her drink. "No, thank you. You might be hot as fuck, but that would be a hard pass. I'm not getting married. *Ever*."

"Whoa there, tiger. I was just kidding. No need to get all flustered." I reach over the bar and grab some extra napkins, handing them to her with a smile. "Tell me, how does a gorgeous woman such as yourself come to know the quirks of Sinatra's drinking habits?"

She takes the napkins and starts dabbing at her dress. "Long story short, I worked at a blues bar in Lakewood. They used to have a Sinatra night once a week. Sinatra drinks, Sinatra music, and even his favorite foods. One of my regulars made sure to school me on everything Sinatra." With a wink and a smile, she takes a finger and taps it to her temple. "It's all up here."

Well shit, could this girl get any more perfect? Reaching out, I stroke her arm with the back of my hand. Immediately, goose bumps rise across her creamy skin, letting me know my touch affects her.

"Why'd you do that?" A flush spreads across her beautiful face and I can't help but envision her doing that very thing, underneath me, in my bed.

I blink slow and hard. What is this woman doing to me? I never take women back to my place. It's always their pad or a penthouse suite at The Pearl.

"Well, are you going to answer my question or are you going to keep staring, taking it to next-level creeper status?" She raises a brow as if annoyed but the smirk on her lips lets me know she's still in this.

"Making sure you're real. For a second there I thought I must be dreaming." I shoot her a shy smile. *Another unusual reaction on my part.* There isn't a shy bone in my body, yet this woman makes me feel like a schoolboy crushing on a girl for the first time. "Sorry. I'm not usually like this. You've sort of caught me off-guard." *Real smooth, Ren. Why don't you just hand over your balls while you're at it?*

"It's okay. I think it's kind of cute."

"Cute, huh? Does cute buy me the privilege of knowing your name?"

In front of her, she spins a coaster displaying an ad for Angel vodka. With a smirk, she finally answers, "It's Angel."

This woman might have me messed up, but I wasn't born yesterday. *It's cool. It's all good.* I silently repeat to myself. Maybe if I say it enough, it'll actually be true.

Normally a woman wanting to keep her true identity private wouldn't bother me one bit but that's definitely not the case with 'Angel.' I *need* to know who she is. Who she *really* is.

"So, *Angel*—what do you like to do for fun?"

"Listen, let's cut the bullshit and get to the meat of it." She snickers to herself, laughing at her inside joke. "You've been eye-fucking me since you stepped into my personal space, so it's clear that what's on your mind isn't what I like to do for fun." Her eyes glitter with mischief as she bites her plump lower lip. "If you tell me what you really want, I might just give it to you."

ACTS OF SALVATION

My brows knit together as my lips part in disbelief. *Where has this woman been hiding?* "Okay. What I really want is to take you out for dinner. Renzetti's down the street is open until two, so how about I close out your tab and we head out now."

"Sorry. I don't *do* dates and that sounds an awful lot like a date."

"Okay then, what do you do if not dinner?"

"*You.*" Angel reaches her hand out and lightly trails it up the inside of my thigh. If her words hadn't clued me in on what she wanted, then her hungry gaze most certainly would. She looks like she's about to devour me whole—and to be honest, I wouldn't mind it one bit.

Angel slips a card into my pocket before getting up from her seat and placing two twenties onto the bar. Bringing her face close to mine, she whispers, "Room 111 at The Pearl. See you in twenty."

I try to clear my throat but my vocal cords fail me, keeping me from getting a single word out. Before I know it, Angel has left the bar with only her intoxicating scent lingering in her wake.

Fuck. Fuck. Fuuuuuuck.

My phone displays four a.m. as I quietly make my way out of the hotel room. I *never* stay this late with a hookup, much less fall asleep in their arms. *Their toned and very strong arms...* My mind drifts off to memories of last night when those arms held me up as we tried unimaginable positions, only made possible by my lover's incredible strength.

I roll my eyes at myself. *He is not your lover, Cassie.*

That man is dangerous to both my mental and physical health. I'll be sore for a week—minimum—the lingering sensation taunting me with what I'll never have again.

That was *the* best sex of my life and there's no doubt in my mind that if I let him into my bed just one more time, I'll turn into a dick-whipped shell of a woman, following him around like a love-struck puppy.

Yes, dick-whipped is a thing. *In fact,* I come from a long line of dick-whipped women. Once they're struck, they're down for the count.

Don't believe me? Just ask my sister, Carmen, who instead of pursuing her dreams, caters to her man's every wish and desire.

Or my sister, Aria, who flushed her full ride at Stanford down the drain in order to follow her *fiancé* around the country.

And let's not forget the OG of being dick-whipped—my mother, Catalina.

Nope. That won't be me. Not if I can help it.

His pull might be strong—hell, I even broke some of my own rules—but I still managed to leave without giving him my real name or number. That should be enough to ensure I never see him again.

Guilt niggles at the back of my mind as I get into my jeep, but I shove it away, telling myself we both knew what this was. *A one-night stand.*

Needing to put as much distance between me and this growing sense of emptiness, I turn the key and start the engine, retreating from the mystery man that's caused it.

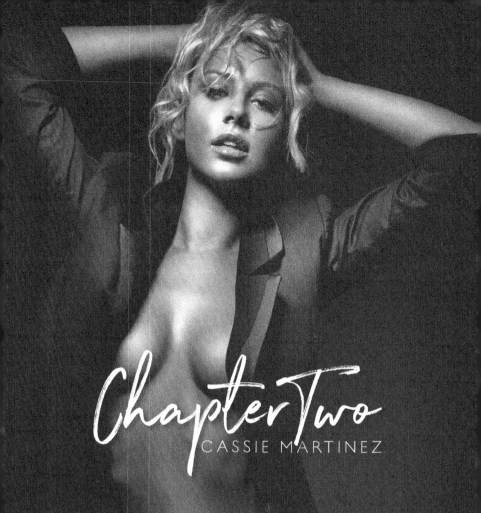

Chapter Two
CASSIE MARTINEZ

IT'S BEEN FOUR DAYS since experiencing the most amazing sex of my life. It's *totally* normal to still be having flashbacks—*totally*. I'm sure that with time, the vivid flashes of toned and tanned flesh flexing above and below me will fade away.

Time. That's all I need.

"You still with me, Cass?" Bella's brows scrunch together as the corner of her mouth lifts into a smirk.

I blink long and hard, trying to scrub the visions of my mystery man away. "Yea, sorry. I was thinking of the new fall line coming out in a couple of weeks." I pick up the two glasses of iced tea I just poured and head over to the living area of my loft apartment while Bella lets out a squeal.

"Does that mean you're hooking a girl up?" Bella's face beams as she pets Bruce, my massive cane corso. He's obsessed with Bella, or any other female for that matter, but hates anything with a cock. Makes for an awesome guard dog, which comes in handy seeing as I don't live in the best of neighborhoods.

Deep Ellum might be trendy, but there are some sketch mofos out at night.

"Of course." I smile as I shake my head at Bruce's shamelessness. "Should I schedule you for a slot at Louvier's?"

"Yes, please!" Bella does a little happy dance in her chair. "I love having a personal shopper as a bestie."

"Well, it *is* how we met." I chuckle before taking a sip of my iced tea, remembering the first time Bella walked into our department store, as clueless and color-blind as they come.

"How could I ever forget. You saved me from myself!" Bella rolls her eyes at the memory. "Speaking of saving me… Dad is hosting a party at the house this weekend and I *need* you to be there."

"You know I don't do parties, Bella. At least not *those* kinds of parties." I lift a brow and purse my lips. Bella should know better than to invite me to one of her fancy shindigs.

She comes from old money, lives on a massive estate in the middle of Highland Park, and is used to being a socialite. Me? I've always felt awkward and out of place in her world, and trust me, I've been in it plenty.

Growing up, Mom held various jobs and most of them revolved

ACTS OF SALVATION

around catering to the uber wealthy. I'd say about ninety percent of the time her employers were egotistical and power hungry, not giving a damn about how their actions would impact those who loyally served them.

The only reason I ended up becoming best friends with Bella is because, despite her wallet, she is nothing like your typical rich Dallas snob. She's kind and caring, always putting her loved ones' needs before her own. She's a true gem.

"But this is different," she pleads with big puppy dog eyes. "It's super low-key. Just a backyard barbeque. We can chill by the pool, sip on margaritas, work on our tans..." She waggles her perfectly groomed brows. "Doesn't that sound like fun?"

Bella is well aware of my aversion to the Dallas elite. Ironic, seeing as how it's my job to dress and style them—but, this *does* sound like fun. "You promise it's going to be chill?"

Bella's face lights up, realizing I might actually be giving in for once. "Yes. Super chill. Small group of people, grilling, pool, and margs."

"Okay, fine. But if I end up feeling awkward, it'll be the *first* and *last* time I attend one of your events."

"Eeeep! You'll finally get to meet my dad and uncle" Bella claps in excitement. "I can't believe we've known each other for over a year and you still haven't met my family."

My cell buzzes on the coffee table and I see it's my mom. "Speaking of family..." I reach for the phone, bringing it to my ear once I've answered. "Mami? Everything okay? You never call me during the day."

"Si, Cassandra. Everything is fine. I was just seeing if you could stop by the house. I made flan," she singsongs that last bit, knowing her desserts are my weakness.

"Sure, Mom. Bella is over right now but I can head over in like an hour." I'm about to hang up when I remember to shout a warning, "And don't let anyone else eat my flan!"

My mom chuckles into the receiver, "Okay. See you soon, *mija*."

"Everything okay?" Bella's concerned eyes are watching me intently. Despite only having known each other a short while, she knows me pretty well and doesn't miss much.

"Yeah, I'm not sure. Mom said everything's good but I have a sneaking suspicion something's up."

An hour and a half later I'm walking up to Mom's one-bedroom home in Oak Cliff. It's a tiny bungalow style building with decorative metal bars across the windows and doors. The *decorative* part is designed to help make the security bars feel less oppressive, but I see them for what they really are—the wardens of my youth and the keepers of its secrets.

Immediately upon opening the door I'm assaulted by the delicious aromas coming from the kitchen. I quickly make my way past the small living room, bypassing the massive portrait of the Virgin Mary, ready to stare me down with judging eyes. *Not today, Mary. Not today.*

"In here!" Mom shouts.

ACTS OF SALVATION

As soon as I step foot into the tiny galley kitchen, I see that she's been extremely busy—seemingly cooking the entire contents of her refrigerator.

"What's all this?" I wave my hands toward the copious amounts of food.

"Well I have to cook everything before they turn the power off. You need to take some of this home with you and stick it in your freezer." She doesn't look me in the eyes as she says this, just continues to stir whatever she has on the stove. "Your sisters will be over later to pick up the rest so you get first dibs."

"Ma... Why are they turning the power off?" My chest vibrates with silent rage, waiting for an explanation, even though I'm pretty sure I already know what it is.

Slowly, Mom turns to finally look me in the eye. "Your father..." But looks away before continuing. "He took everything before he left." Mom wipes at her face and sniffs. "He even cleared out my emergency stash." She walks toward the cupboard, retrieving an innocuous coffee can only to open it and show me it's missing its contents.

Now isn't the time to point out that a coffee can isn't the safest spot to hide money. Instead I take two steps forward and pull Mom into my arms. "Everything will be okay, Ma. The girls and I will pool together with what we can. We'll figure this out."

"Since when did you turn into the grown-up?" Mom half sobs, half chuckles into me.

'*The day I decided I wouldn't let love make me a fool,*' I think to myself as I let out a tired sigh. I keep this to myself of course. There's no way I'm rubbing salt in Mom's fresh wound.

Today's events have poured over me like an ice-cold bucket of water. If I had any lingering doubts about my mystery man and his deliciously toned body, this disaster right here serves as the perfect reminder of why I never get romantically involved.

As I mentally pat myself on the back, I *know* I made the right call.

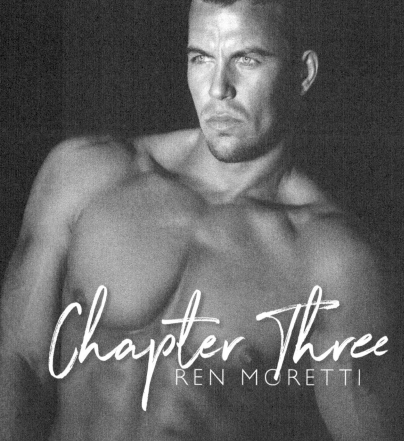

Chapter Three
REN MORETTI

I ROLL UP TO MY BROTHER'S house and note that all the usual cars are here with the new addition of William's black Range Rover. Now that he's single, he can start coming to our get-togethers again.

Poor schmuck. His ex, Heather, sucked the life right out of him. I swear, if you looked up the definition for a soul-sucking demon you'd probably see Heather's picture.

Naturally, being his best friend, it's my job to get him back on the straight and narrow… aka lots and lots of sex.

Sex. The mere word conjures up images of Angel, the beautiful blond I met last weekend. No matter how hard I try, she's always in the forefront of my mind. Whether it's the delicious way she writhed underneath me or the ridiculous amounts of Sinatra trivia she impressed me with, she's always there, popping up at all hours of the day.

I roll my eyes as I make my way through Aiden's palatial home. *I wonder what Angel would think of Aiden's ostentatious abode.* It's such a waste of space if you ask me.

There are only four people living here—my brother, niece, and twin nephews—yet this 'house' boasts twelve rooms, a gym, a bowling alley, a tennis court, and an indoor/outdoor pool. A bit of overkill if you ask me.

The hot summer air hits me as I step out into the backyard. Music plays over the outdoor speakers and the area is decked with various food and beverage stations spread throughout. To my right there's a massive metal trough full of ice which holds an assortment of adult beverages as well as bottles of water.

A little past the drinks is the cabana and outdoor kitchen where Aiden is manning the grill as he talks to a brunette. A brunette who's eying him like he's her next meal. Chuckling, I decide to catch up with my brother later. It seems he has his hands full at the moment.

Grabbing a couple of beers out of the trough, I head over to William and Titus by the pool. As I approach the two I see their attention is focused on the two women stationed right across from them, my niece Bella and possibly one of her friends.

"Watcha lookin' at?" Titus shoves at William's shoulder, a wide grin splaying across his face.

I narrow my eyes at William. "You've got that same look you did at the bar last week. Too bad the ladies by the pool are off-limits." I let out a chuckle before getting serious and cocking a brow. "*Especially* my niece."

"You're off your rocker, Ren. I'm not interested in Bella or her friend. I was just in my head, thinking of a new contract I'm trying to pull in." William tries to remain passive, but I can tell my words have gotten to him. He's been so tense lately, but I mean who could blame him with everything he's got going on.

"*Sure*. That's what that look of desire was all about. Your desire for a new contract." I roll my eyes as I hand him one of the beers I'd been holding.

Titus lets out a low whistle. "They have tight little bodies. I wouldn't fault you for looking."

I'm about to smack him for talking about my eighteen-year-old niece like that when my eyes land on Bella's friend. Bella's very beautiful and *blond* friend. A friend that looks an awful lot like Angel…

The pounding of my heart throbs in my head, effectively muffling all the noise around me. Could *my* Angel be friends with Bella? *Fuck*. Does that mean she's Bella's age? I'm thirty-two—almost a decade and a half older!

William's barely audible voice buzzes in the background, but the word blond has me tuning back in. "…how'd it go with the blond you set your sights on, Ren? I haven't heard you talk about anyone since. Has the eternal bachelor finally settled down?"

His words sucker punch me in the gut, making me spit out the swig of beer I just took into my mouth. *Fuck*. That's most definitely Angel.

"Whoa there, buddy." William taps me on the back. "What happened?"

"Beer went down the wrong pipe… I think big bro might need some help manning the grill. See y'all later." I spin on my heels, needing to avoid William's inquisition. There's no way I'd be able to live it down if he found out the very blond he'd just asked about was my niece's teenage friend.

I need to get out of dodge, and fast.

As I approach Aidan in the cabana I notice that he's looking rather uncomfortable. That's extremely odd because Aiden *never* shows discomfort. As an ex-Navy SEAL, he's all about keeping his cards close to his vest and never displaying emotion. It's why he's the lead on most of our high-profile contracts. Granted, most of the people who hire our private security firm are notable, but if it's a high-risk case with notoriety then Aiden gets first dibs.

"*Fratellino.*" Aiden's eyes find me, immediately displaying a sense of relief as he calls me brother in our native tongue. I can tell he's happy to use me as an excuse to get out of the situation he's in, and I don't blame him one bit.

This cougar has clearly set her eyes on him and if there's one thing I know about my brother, it's that he's still hung up on his dead wife.

It's been three years and the man has yet to go on one date.

"You remember Mariana, my wife's sister?" Aiden cocks a brow as he reintroduces me to the brunette.

"Oh yeah… I thought you looked familiar. I believe the last time I saw you was at the funeral. Excuse my memory. That was a very emotional day for all of us." I purse my lips to the side trying to figure out why Mariana would be hitting on her deceased sister's husband.

"I wish I could be around more for the kids but working with

ACTS OF SALVATION

the Bureau keeps me extremely busy, always traveling and never in one place for long." Mariana bats her lashes up at me as she places a hand on my chest, not so discretely stroking the muscles underneath.

And just like that, it becomes clear. This woman will hit on anything with a cock.

Smirking, I lift her hand off my chest. "Yes. I understand it must get extremely lonely. Would you excuse us? I would like a word with my brother." Ever since being with Angel, the thought of any other woman just feels wrong—even if it's just harmless flirting—the sooner she's gone, the better.

"Oh, of course. I think I'll go check on the twins." Mariana feigns a blush as she saunters off to the kiddie play area where all the adults dropped off their offspring upon arrival. Gotta give it to Aiden—or more likely Bella—for thinking of everything. They even hired child care so that the grown-ups could relax without having to stress about what their kids were doing.

"Thanks for the save," Aiden mutters under his breath. "Can you believe the balls on that one?" He motions toward Mariana's retreating frame.

"Awe. She's just lonely, Brother." I laugh, knowing I've probably set him off with that. Wanting to stop any verbal sparring session, I quickly cut into his thoughts. "So… who's that with Bella?" I point my beer bottle toward the gorgeous blond whom I'm pretty positive is Angel.

"Huh?" Aiden looks up from the grill and toward the pool. "Oh, that's Cassie. Isabella's new bestie." He makes a face before continuing. "*Bestie*. Kids these days. They shorten everything."

Cassie. Her name echoes in my mind.

25

"How come I haven't seen her before? You know, since they're 'besties' and all." Taking a sip of my beer I turn to my brother. I need to know more about Cassie but I don't want to come off overly interested.

"No clue. You'd have to ask her." Aidan raises a brow. "Why?"

Shit. I need to shake the bloodhound off my trail. "No reason, just wondering."

Aiden purses his lips to the side. "Uh-huh. Well, like I said, you'll have to ask her." He quickly gives me side-eye before returning his attention to the grill.

Oh, I plan to little angel.

Cassie

I'm making my way back into this palatial home in search of the bathroom when someone calling my name stops me dead in my tracks. "*Cassie.*"

That deep baritone voice has me slowly spinning around. I'd recognize it anywhere, seeing how it's the one that haunts me every single second of every single day.

"*Bella mia.*" The beautiful stranger walks up to me, lifting the back of his hand and running it along the bare skin of my arm, just as he had the first night we met. "Where you off to?"

"You must have me confused. Bella is over by the pool." I motion toward my best friend, lying on the lounge chair where I left her. I need to shake this man, and fast. Never in a million years

ACTS OF SALVATION

would I have thought that the very subject of my fantasies would be in my best friend's home. *What are the odds?*

He chuckles. His laugh sending a ripple of desire through me as I remember it in the context of our one *amazing* night together. He opens his mouth to speak and the next words that come out leave me absolutely floored, "I'm not confused, my beautiful *Angel*. I was calling you 'my beautiful' in Italian, and I *definitely* wasn't talking about my niece, Bella."

My breath halts as his words suck the air out of me. "Your... *niece?*" My eyes practically bug out of my head.

Okay, if I thought seeing him here was random, the fact that the man I've been lusting over for the past week is my best friend's uncle seems to take the cake.

Not a second later, this gorgeous man has me pinned against the house, his large palms bracing my back and pulling me into him.

"Cassie," he groans, his breath tickling the soft skin of my neck as he breathes me in, causing me to shudder in his arms.

This man has a hold on me I can't explain and I find myself helpless against his magnetic pull.

"Yes?" my voice comes out a ragged whisper.

Running his nose down my neck, his luscious lips pepper wet kisses along my skin, leaving goose bumps in their wake. "God, I've missed you, *little angel*." His eyes sear into mine, flickering back and forth, seemingly as confused and overwhelmed with emotion as mine.

He begins to lower his face, hovering his lips over my begging mouth when Bella's voice breaks into our little bubble of lust. Her laugh serving as an ice-cold bucket of reality, temporarily dousing any desire right out of me.

"Yes, I'll be there. I promise." Bella appears as she turns the corner leading to the back yard. "Okay, I'll call if anything changes." Removing the phone from her ear, Bella looks up at me and then her uncle, who'd reluctantly released me upon hearing her voice.

He stands a couple of feet away from me bearing a tortured look on his face.

"Uncle Ren? What are you doing back here…" Bella shifts her gaze back and forth between us. "with Cassie?"

"He was just helping me find the bathroom." I give her an awkward laugh, hoping she's buying what I'm selling. "But now that you're here, you can help me." I grab her arm and drag her the rest of the way into the home, not daring to look back at the man who's managed to snake his way into my every waking thought.

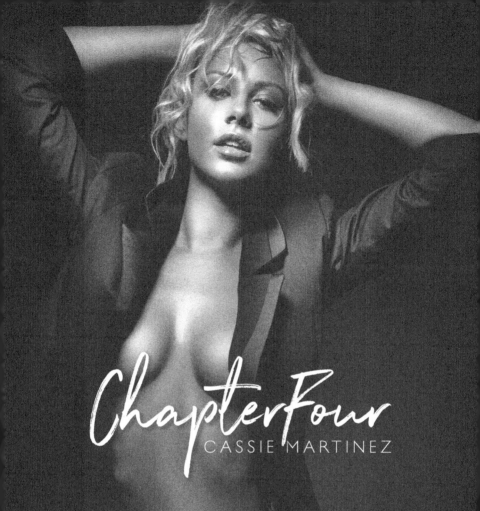

Chapter Four
CASSIE MARTINEZ

THE OVERSIZED SUNGLASSES taunt me from their display, with their ultra-dark frames and their potential to hide what lies underneath.

I got little to no sleep last night and the bags under my eyes show it. I so wish I could just slip a pair of those gorgeous black frames on and fly incognito for the rest of the day but unfortunately that isn't on my schedule.

Instead I swing by the complimentary coffee bar and pick up a double shot of espresso, tipping Marcus on the way up to the top floor of our flagship store in downtown Dallas. I have a big client coming in today and I can't afford to mess this up. I need all the money I can get my hands on since it looks like I'll be needing to front some of Mom's bills again.

Dad has yet to rear his ugly head and I'm pretty certain he isn't going to until he's blown through all of Mom's money.

My phone buzzes as I make my way past the designer gowns and into the private dressing rooms. Looking down I notice it's an unknown number. *Hmmm.* I hit unlock and what I see makes my breath hitch.

UNKNOWN NUMBER: We should talk. - Ren

I shut my eyes as if doing so will somehow make the message disappear. *Ren.* My best friend's uncle, *Ren.* The man I can't seem to get out of my head, *Ren.* The man I have no business talking to, *Ren.*

Luckily I don't have much time to drown in my thoughts as my client, Blair, calls my name bringing me back to the here and now.

"Daaarling, it's been too long." She brings her hands to mine, blowing an air kiss on either cheek before retreating to her personal space. "We're going on vacation next week and we need new everything."

"Wonderful!" I muster a smile at the promise of a big pay out. "Will the family be coming in for a fitting or shall we go based on their sizes from their last visit?"

"Neither." Blair twirls a short lock of hair as she purses her lips and squints. "Well I was sort of hoping you could stop by the house with your options for the family. And now that we're discussing you stopping by the house, I was also wondering if there was a way I could entice you to be our own personal stylist."

My brows scrunch together in confusion, "*Personal stylist?*"

Blair's face lights up as she steps closer before whispering, "Yes. As in you'd only be working for me and my family." Her cold hand slips a card into mine. "Here's the figure we'd be willing to pay. Don't give me an answer now. Think about it and then get back to me." She cocks a brow before resuming her distance once more.

I'm pretty certain she knows it's against store policy to poach a personal shopper for herself, but she doesn't seem to care about the ramifications. Me, on the other hand, I could get blacklisted. It's a pretty big risk to put all of your eggs in one basket.

I discreetly look down at the card and my eyes bug out at the number—it's almost *double* the amount I make at the department store. That makes it extremely tempting but I can't afford to take the risk. If for some reason things don't work out, I'd not only be out of a job, but no department store would hire me after wronging *Louvier's*.

Turning to face the very blond, and very hopeful Blair, I smile and give her a small nod. "I'll think about it." My words are short but offer her a sliver of hope, no sense in destroying today's chances for a sale, right?

"Perfect. That's all that I ask." Blair runs her fingers along a beautiful wrap dress I've pulled for her. "Let's start with this one, shall we?"

Back at my loft, I'm greeted by Bruce. His massive paws reach up to my shoulders as he stands on his hind legs, giving me extra kisses and affection. He always seems to know when I need cheering up.

"Hey, buddy. Did you miss Mommy?" I scratch behind his ears before pulling his paws off me and heading toward his treat jar. "What will it be today, biscuit or jerky?"

My purse begins to vibrate as Bruce contemplates his choices. Reaching in to pull my phone out I see it's a message from my sister, Aria.

ARIA: **Hey, stopped by Mom's this afternoon and saw the eviction notice her landlord was serving her as I left. She's too proud to take money from us directly, but if we all pull together, we can pay the landlord ourselves. You in?**

CASSIE: Of course. Count me in.

ARIA: **Awesome. I'll be by your place in the morning.**

Tallying up all of Mom's bills, my stomach churns. I have a little in savings but helping out will eat right through it and then some. There's no question that I'm going to help with all that I have, but it doesn't take away the sting and anger rolling through me.

My fucking father… Well, more like my mother falling for my *fucking* father.

And this is exactly why I won't be answering Ren's text

ACTS OF SALVATION

message. Men make women stupid. An adage as sure as time itself. At least I think it's an adage? Well, if it isn't, it definitely needs to be.

I roll my eyes as I slump against the kitchen counter, reaching across and opening the freezer to pull out the vodka. *It's martini time.*

Tossing my phone back into my purse, it lands on the card Blair handed me earlier today. The figure stares back at me, mocking me with the promise of financial security—something I've never had.

Fuck it. If there was ever a reason to risk everything it would be for my family. Picking up the card and phone, I shoot a message to Blair.

CASSIE: I accept.

Two dangerous little words, with so much potential. Potential that isn't all good.

Not a moment later, I see the telltale little dots bouncing across the screen letting me know a response is coming.

BLAIR: **Fantastic! Please stop by the house tomorrow. We'll have your contract ready and waiting.**
1111 Sheridan Ct.
Highland Park, Texas 75205

As I read over her message, I decide to pour myself a double, needing the liquid courage to seal this deal with the devil.

The devil wears Prada, indeed.

Chapter Five
CASSIE MARTINEZ

I'M STANDING IN FRONT of a massive French-style chateau smack dab in the middle of one of *the* most pretentious neighborhoods in Dallas. To say my skin is crawling would be an understatement.

Don't get me wrong, I don't hate luxury, I love a gorgeous pair of Jimmy Choo's just as much as the next girl—I just hate the condescending and entitled behavior that typically comes with those who can afford it.

The door swings open and a matronly woman with gray hair up in a twist appears. "Good afternoon, Ms. Martinez. The family is waiting in the lounge." She motions me into the home, looking behind me she quickly adds, "Will you be needing assistance with anything?"

"Yes, please. If someone could help bring in the trolly with the garment bags and boxes that would be wonderful. Thank you."

Last night Blair gave me access to one of her cards. I was able to shop for her and her family, pulling anything they might need for their trip. Whatever they don't like I can just return or exchange.

The perks of being a personal stylist, you get to shop on someone else's dime. The con, the stuff isn't yours to keep.

"Daaarling, I can't wait to see what you've got for us!" Blair greets me from behind the bar, discreetly tucked into the corner of the lounge. It looks like she's just poured herself a glass of white wine. "You remember my husband, Dr. Woodrow Wilson, and our children, Penelope and Thomas, right?"

I look around the room and see her husband in an Eames lounge chair, so out of place with the rest of the French decor. Upon hearing his name, Dr. Wilson looks up from his phone and when his eyes meet mine—something in them flickers, too quickly for me to discern. Within a second he's back to his aloof self, staring back at his phone.

Okay, that was weird.

Looking toward the other end of the room, I notice the children for the first time. They've been so quiet I wouldn't have known they were in the room were it not for Blair's introduction. Sitting at a kid-size table, they are fully engrossed in whatever they have going on in their tablets, oblivious to the world around them.

This whole scene is sort of creepy. Everyone seems so detached from each other.

ACTS OF SALVATION

My family might be dysfunctional, but our home has always been full of laughter and love. This home is more a reproduction of a still life portrait, and it gives me the heebie-jeebies.

"Since I just poured myself this drink, why don't you start off with Woodrow. He seems to need the most help anyway." Blair lifts a brow as she takes a sip.

Woodrow seemingly unaffected by his wife's shade simply gets up from his chair, places his phone in his pocket, and walks past me before looking back. "Shall we?" He motions toward the hall.

"I was hoping we could go over the pieces here, and then you could try on anything you liked." I clear my throat, waiting for his answer. The idea of being alone with this man has me on edge. I can't quite place my finger on it but there is something off about him.

"Nonsense. I'm not going to *drop trou* here in the middle of the lounge. Besides, if we go to my bedroom then you'll get to see my closet and all the clothes in it. It'll give you a better sense of my style."

"Or lack thereof..." Blair mumbles into her wine glass.

Woodrow, completely ignoring his wife's disparaging remark, continues walking. "Just point to the boxes and bags that are mine and Winslow will take them to the room."

As if on cue, a white-haired man appears, immediately standing next to the pile I'd brought with me. "Which items will it be, miss?"

Of course, they'd have a butler.

Hesitating a moment before agreeing, I begin to point out the items intended for Blair's husband before following the man himself into the hallway.

The entire home is museum status worthy. Not a spec of dirt to be seen and everything from the decor to the finishes screams money, and not in a gaudy way either.

Woodrow stops in front of a door, "This is Blair's bedroom, and mine is just down the hall." He begins walking once more, leaving me with a ton of questions.

Why do they have separate rooms? That seriously can't be healthy for their love life. And why did he so blatantly point out Blair's room? It's not like she wouldn't have shown me where it was later...

I don't have time to ruminate over my questions because before we know it, we've arrived at Woodrow's door.

"After you." He steps aside, letting me through first.

My jaw just about hits the floor upon entering. Closing my mouth quickly, I try and recover. This room makes Bella's look like the peasants' quarters.

There's a massive four-poster bed front and center, complete with drapery, King Henry the 8th style. Come to think of it, everything in this room is of the same Tudor style—from the bed down to the lighting. Even the ceiling is arched and delineated with massive dark brown beams.

"I know... It doesn't exactly go with the rest of the home." Woodrow chuckles from behind me. "It's the only room I could fully take control of... It's the only room that is *completely* Blair free." He slowly edges closer to me with that last statement, putting me further on edge.

Okay. If he'd put me on edge before, he's full-on freaking me the fuck out now. I keep stepping backward until the back of my knees hit his bed.

"Has anyone ever told you how beautiful you are?" The creeper keeps walking toward me, completely unaware or uncaring of my discomfort.

I quickly sidestep toward the massive opening which I presume is either his restroom or his closet, needing to put some serious space between us.

"I see you've noticed my closet." The man appears behind me as if performing some sort of Houdini act. *How's he so fast?!*

"Yes, it's gorgeous," I squeak, trying to keep the nerves out of my voice but failing miserably. "Okay, now that I have a good sense of your style, why don't you step into the bathroom and try on the first couple of items Winslow just placed on your bed."

Thank the Lord for the butler. He walked in at the right time. Not sure what Creeper McCreeperson would have tried had we not been interrupted.

"Of course." Woodrow clears his throat as he steps back into the bedroom, grabbing a couple of bags before heading into the bathroom.

As soon as the bathroom door closes, the one to the hall opens and Blair steps in.

My head spins at this door version of musical chairs. *Can't I just get a moment to collect myself?*

"Cassie, I forgot to hand you this when you arrived. It's the contract and we've even gone ahead and added a signing bonus." A self-satisfied smirk ghosts her lips.

I look down and the bonus itself is enough to send me stumbling back, but I'm not about to give her the satisfaction of watching me react. I'm sure to her this is chump change, but to me, twenty thousand dollars is an absurd amount.

Immediately my mother comes to mind. "I'll look it over and

get back to you."

Blair attempts to look confused but Botox has permanently frozen off most of her natural expression. "But I thought it was a done deal? You said you *agreed.*"

I know it's probably not the best idea to piss off your potential new employer, but I'm not one-hundred percent certain I want to sell my soul to the devil just yet—especially with Creeper McCreeperson being part of the packaged deal.

"Thinking about it now, I figured we could do sort of a trial run. If everything goes well, then I'll most likely sign."

"Oh, they *will* go well. And you *will* sign." She purses her lips and attempts to raise her brows, trying to look fierce, but instead achieves the look of a constipated teenager with duck lips.

Looking up toward the vaulted ceiling I send up a silent prayer, hoping for clarity on whether or not I should take a dive into this pool of money and crazy.

God, I hope it's all worth it.

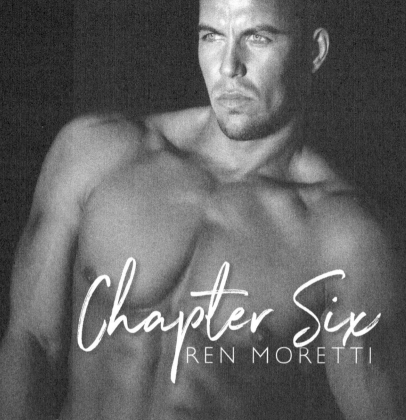

Chapter Six
REN MORETTI

I CANT GET ASSIE OUT OF MY HEAD. Despite knowing that I could never pursue anything with her, visions of her naked body and wild eyes keep flitting around in my brain. One time with her was enough to sear her into my soul.

I've just arrived at William's place to go over a contract and instead of being excited about the new client I landed, I'm over here thinking of Cassie and her luscious lips. The way her smile lights up her face. The story behind her hazel eyes. Those eyes...

There's so much history in those eyes. You can tell she's lived a full life, unsheltered and raw, experiencing every emotion but keeping every single one close to her chest.

Stepping out of the car and up to William's home, I mentally shake myself. This is *not* the time to be thinking about a girl. And that's what she is. A teenage girl. Certainly not someone I need to be fantasizing about.

The door swings open and my breath halts. *Did I just conjure this girl up?*

"Ren?" Cassie squints her eyes as if unsure of what she's seeing. "What are you doing here?"

"I was just about to ask you the same thing." I step inside, inhaling her unique scent as I walk past her. "But hey, I won't look a gift horse in the mouth."

Whatever's brought her here, I'm not questioning.

"Well since you're here, mind keeping an eye on this?" She hands me a monitor where baby Harper is napping in what appears to be her crib. "I need to get something from my car and I'm not sure the baby monitor gets good reception outside."

"Sure, no problem." I smile like a fool as she steps outside, softly closing the door behind her.

Turning around, I head to the kitchen, needing to fix myself something to eat. I didn't eat lunch and was planning on grabbing dinner with William—but that doesn't look very likely now.

I whip out my phone to text the man in question.

REN: Hey, I stopped by your place to go over the new contract, but you aren't here.

WILLIAM: Oh shit, sorry man. Forgot to tell you, I had a last-minute dinner with a potential

ACTS OF SALVATION

client. Won't be home until late tonight. Let's go over it in the morning.

REN: **No worries. See you then.**

I'm putting my phone back in my pocket when Cassie steps into the kitchen. "I see why you're babysitting now. William is out at a client dinner."

Cassie makes a strangled sound as she places some papers on the counter. "Uh-huh. That's it, alright."

I furrow my brows. "What I don't get is why you're here instead of Bella. Isn't she taking care of Harper?"

"Ummm, yeah. She had something come up." Cassie points to the bread in my hand. "It looks like you're hungry. Why don't you let me fix you something real quick?"

"You won't catch me saying no to that! I love to eat but I can't cook worth shit." I let out a laugh.

"Well, I love to cook. After a long day, there's nothing better than pouring myself a drink, playing a little music, and getting lost in the art of food."

I stare at this woman, losing myself in the way she moves as she speaks, her face and hands expressively conveying every inflection of her tone. Then it hits me... "Wait, how old are you? Are you even old enough to drink?"

Cassie rolls her eyes. "I'm old enough to drink in the UK, and most every other country except for this one."

"So that makes you what..."

"Nineteen. I'm nineteen." Cassie lets out an exasperated breath before arching a brow, begging me to argue the fact that she's too young to be drinking. But all my brain can wrap itself around is the fact that she's still a teenager.

I've been lusting after a goddamned teenager.

Realizing I'm not going to add to the conversation right now, Cassie turns around and opens the Sub-Zero fridge. It's fully stocked with fresh veggies and proteins. No snacks to be seen.

"William is a health freak. Usually has Chef prep his lunches for the week so he doesn't have to eat out." I shake my head before continuing. "Me, the greasier the better."

"My kind of cooking." Cassie winks as she produces a couple of bone-in pork chops from the fridge, placing them on the counter before disappearing into the pantry.

Looking down on the counter, I see the papers she'd brought in earlier. It looks like some sort of contract. Wow, it's for a decent amount of money. Good for her.

"What are you doing?" Cassie scrunches her face as she places a bag of potatoes in the sink. "That's personal."

"I've had my cock in almost every hole of your body. I'd say that's pretty personal."

The look of indignation on her face is priceless. I want to kiss it right off, but instead of addressing my brand of humor, Cassie redirects. "It's a contract... for a job I might be taking."

The hesitation in her voice makes me worry. "Why do you sound so unsure? It seems like a great opportunity on paper. Well, from what I've read so far."

"The client's husband. He's sort of a creep."

Immediately my whole body tenses. The thought of some creep perving on what's mine sets off my adrenaline, needing to protect Cassie from perceived and unperceived dangers alike. I don't even realize what I'm doing until Cassie places her palms on my chest and begins to push me off.

In the span of a minute, I'd walked up to her, pulled her into me, and held on for dear life. *Jesus, what the fuck is wrong with me?* I've never reacted like this over a woman. It's like I'm a different man when it comes to her.

"Sorry, I didn't mean to crowd your personal space. I just couldn't stand the thought of another man going near you like that." I take a reluctant step away from her. "For some irrational reason, I feel that you belong to me—but from your reaction, I'm guessing the feeling isn't mutual."

A pained look flashes across her face, but it's gone in an instant. "I think it's for the best if we keep our distance. Romantically, at least. With you being Bella's uncle and all, and me being her best friend, I'm just not seeing how it could end well."

"Sure." The one word is the only thing I'm able to muster. Her words make sense, but they don't diminish the burn they leave behind. "Why don't you leave the contract with me. I can run a full check on this douche and see if there's any history that would indicate if he'd be dangerous to work with."

Cassie's face lights up and at that moment I realize there isn't anything I wouldn't do to see that look on her face. The thought is jarring, especially given the fact that she's outright rejected me.

"Thank you! That would make me feel a million times better about this job." She closes the space between us, surprising us both with a spontaneous hug. The moment only lasts a second because as soon as she's realized what she's done, she's right back to distancing herself—putting up those ten-foot walls and securing her perimeter. "And to thank you, I'll be making you one of my specialties. Skillet seared pork chops with rosemary roasted potatoes."

"Sounds delicious." I offer her a feeble smile while thinking... *'all I really want is you.'*

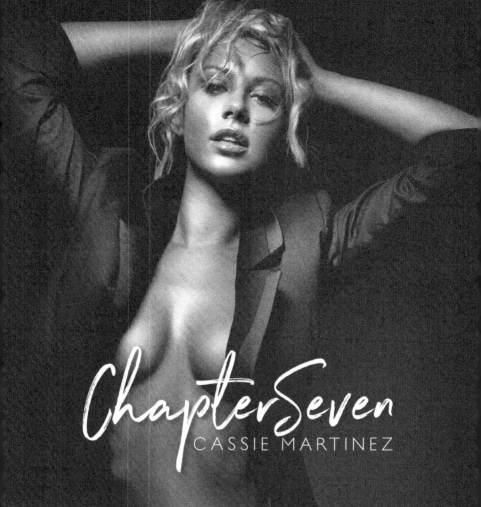

Chapter Seven
CASSIE MARTINEZ

THE WILSON FAMILY LEAVES for their vacation today, and of course, they've left their selections to the very last minute. I'm at their home about to drop off the final pieces they requested when my phone buzzes. I see it's Bella, so of course, I answer.

"Hey, chica. What's up?"

"You busy?" Bella's voice comes out a few octaves higher than usual. *Something's up.*

"I'm at a client's house but I'm never too busy for you. You're my ride or die, girl. So talk to me." It's true, Bella *is* my ride or die—another reason why I could never betray her by dating her uncle. It's already fucked-up enough that I've slept with him.

"I just need some advice. You up for some girl time later?"

"Of course. Meet me at my place in a couple of hours." My mood instantly lifts at the idea of spending a fun night in. Maybe it'll help take my mind off the looming contract and my mother's increasing pile of bills.

"Awesome," Bella singsongs. "I'll bring Torchy's."

"Bless your heart!" I love that she knows me and my penchant for street tacos so well. "Okay, see you later. The butler is waving me in."

"Ooooh, fancy." Bella snickers into the phone.

"Stop. You know your dad would have one too if it wasn't for his ingrained distrust of everyone... Okay, for real now. Bye." I cut the line as I begin to march forward, a rolling cart full of clothes in tow.

Moments later I'm standing in front of Blair, wondering how in the hell I got myself into this mess. "What do you mean?" A bead of sweat rolls down my back at the idea of being alone with Mr. McCreeperson again. "Why can't I just leave Dr. Wilson's selections with you? Aren't you all going to the same place?"

"Yes, darling, of course. But Woodrow has a business dinner before his flight." Blair stares blankly at me as if that should explain everything.

Newsflash, it doesn't.

Demurely huffing out air and rolling her eyes, she continues. "He'll need the Audemars Piguet you special ordered for him from Vegas. Thank you for that, by the way. I know it was the last one on the market and we're very impressed you were able to get your hands on it." Blair purses her lips again, recreating her favorite duck lip pose. "See, this is why we simply must have you as our personal stylist." She circles me like a shark circles its prey. "Have you given the contract any thought? Things are going extremely well, and that bonus is burning a hole in my pocket."

There she goes again, pursing those lips. Wanting to stop any further discussion of the contract, I acquiesce. "Fine. I'll stop by Dr. Wilson's office on my way home. Will I be taking all of his selections or just the watch?"

"Just the watch." Blair claps as if she's won the war.

Just the battle, Blair. Just the battle.

McCreeperson's office is located between Oak Lawn and Turtle Creek. To say that his place of business is swanky would be an understatement.

For fuck's sake, the man has chandeliers in his waiting area. Who needs chandeliers in a waiting area?

"You must be Cassie." A blond woman wearing white scrubs greets me from behind the reception desk. "Could I interest you in some cucumber water while you wait? Dr. Wilson is with a patient right now."

"No, thank you." Of course, they have cucumber water. They probably offer a complimentary massage while you wait. I shake my head at the absurdity.

ELEANOR ALDRICK

Luckily, I don't have to wait long. Woodrow appears from behind a door before I'm able to take a seat in one of their luxurious armchairs.

Trailing behind him is a petite blond woman—*I'm beginning to see a pattern here*—who won't take her eyes off of the good ol' doctor. Her adoration is so intense that she practically runs into Woodrow when he stops abruptly, noticing me for the first time.

"Cassie, what a pleasure." Woodrow directs his attention toward me, completely dismissing his patient, much to her dismay as evidenced by her staring daggers at me.

"Hi." I awkwardly wave, unsure of how to act around him. "Blair asked me to make a special delivery for you." Even though Woodrow's office is flashy, I don't want to come right out and say, 'Hey, I brought you your hundred-thousand-dollar watch.'

"Ah, the watch." The corner of his mouth lifts in a half-smile. "Follow me into my office would you?"

Not really sure why I can't just hand over the box. I'm about to argue the point when the man in question disappears behind the door, leaving me no choice but to follow.

Making my way past several exam rooms, I notice they're all dimly lit with mood music playing within. I have to give it to the man, he certainly knows his clientele.

Snickering to myself, I picture what his ad would be like...

How about a little cucumber mask with your injectables? Here at Dr. McCreeperson's, we've got you covered.

"What's so funny?" Woodrow pulls me out of my thoughts, making me realize I've actually laughed out loud.

"Oh, nothing. So why the need to come back to your office?" I quickly change the subject, not wanting him to know I was laughing at his expense.

"My safe. I wanted to take off the watch I'm wearing now and put it in the safe."

I don't point out that he could have done that without me, or the fact that he'd be sharing the location of his safe by letting me be in here while he accessed it. *Not very smart.*

Before I know it, he's right in front of me, reaching out his hand to brush a strand of hair out of my face. I freeze in horror, completely taken off-guard by his audacity.

"Pardon me saying this but has anybody told you you have the most symmetrical face? It's absolutely stunning. Would have made Nefertiti green with envy." He laughs at his own brand of joke, one I don't think is very funny. If fact, this whole thing is downright creepy.

I try to take a step back but the wall prevents me from moving further. My heart begins to race and my palms sweat from the unexpected proximity to this creep. *Should I knee him in the balls? Slap him and run?*

A vision of the bonus flashes across my mind's eye and it fortifies my resolve to see this trial run through the end. That check could really help Mom, and this weirdo isn't anything I haven't had to handle before.

A faint buzzing breaks the awkward moment and I realize it's my phone. Fishing it out of my bag, I answer, despite not knowing who it is. I need a reprieve from this man and fast.

"Hello?" I rush out before McCreeperson can try anything else.

"Hey girl, where are you? I'm outside your place, but nobody is home?" Bella sounds worried, and rightfully so.

"Hi, yes. I'm not there yet but I will be in like ten minutes. Let yourself in but don't let Bruce have any of my Torchy's I'm not sharing tonight." I give her a weak laugh because it's all I can muster.

Before I've even put away my phone, Woodrow is back in my personal space. "Who's Bruce? Is that your boyfriend?"

Not sure where in the hell this man got the idea that this information is any of his business but I answer him anyway, needing to push him away any way I can. He doesn't need to know that Bruce is actually my hundred-pound dog.

"Yes, he is. And he's at home waiting for me. So if you'll excuse me, I better get going." I slide to the side, escaping the little bubble of tension he had me under.

"I understand. If I had someone as lovely as you, I'd never want to let you out of my sight." Woodrow's brows scrunch together as if it pains him to let me go. This man just keeps getting creepier and creepier.

"Right." Giving him a quick nod, I grab on to the doorjamb, needing to secure my freedom as soon as possible. "Well, you have a wonderful trip."

I turn and speed walk out the door, hightailing it out of there and practically slam into the nurse who'd greeted me earlier.

"Cassie. Is everything alright?" Her super sweet demeanor makes me wonder if she knows what kind of creep she's working for.

Smoothing my hand over my dress, I attempt to recompose myself. "Yes, thank you. Just running late for girls' night."

Clapping her hands together excitedly, the nurse begins to talk a mile a minute. "Oh, that sounds like so much fun. It's been a while since I've had a night out with the girls. Maybe I could tag along?

ACTS OF SALVATION

We don't have any patients for the rest of the day, and I'm sure Dr. Wilson won't mind if I duck out early..." Seeing the look of surprise cross my face, the woman decides to introduce herself. "My name is Barbie, by the way."

It takes a herculean feat to keep myself from snickering. The way she just spoke, all high-pitched, super-fast, and extremely bubbly—let's just say her name suits her perfectly.

"Barbie, that sounds like fun and maybe next time we could make that happen, but my bestie was counting on one-on-one time tonight. You understand, right?"

Blushing profusely, Barbie bobs her head up and down. "Of course, I didn't mean to invite myself like that. It's just that I recently moved here and I don't have that many friends yet."

Now I just feel like a heel. "Okay, how about we grab a coffee sometime soon? Get to know each other more. You might come to realize you don't even like me as a friend." I give Barbie a sheepish smile, hoping she doesn't feel as embarrassed anymore.

"Oh, I'd love that. Thank you." She grabs my hand and squeezes—*wow, Barbie has a grip on her*. "I'll get your number from Dr. Wilson and text you later in the week so we can set that up."

"Sounds good." I give her a quick nod and begin to speed walk away. The last thing I want is for Dr. Wilson to come out of his office and find that I'm still here.

Time to make like a banana and *split*.

Chapter Eight
REN MORETTI

EVEN FIFTEEN-HUNDRED MILES can't keep Cassie out of my head. Despite knowing she's completely friend-zoned me, I can't help but think of her every free moment I get. It's as if she's crawled under my skin and taken up residence in every cell of my being.

I *need* to find a way to stop her from thinking we're a bad idea.

My phone lights up and it's Becca, my secretary. "Hey, any good news?"

"Well, hello to you too, handsome."

"Sorry. Hey, Becca... how are you? Do you have any good

news?"

She cackles. "That's a little better, but not by much. I'm assuming you're wanting to know about the background check you asked me to run—it came back clean. Dr. Wilson is an upstanding citizen, a highly esteemed member of the Texas Medical Board, and adored by all of his patients, per his social media following."

Fuck. I was really wanting to keep this creep away from my girl. But without a valid reason, I'm going to have to get creative.

"Thanks, Becca. Please email me a copy of your findings as soon as possible."

"Already done. So, this rush job. Is there a reason behind it?" Her curious tone has me smiling. *If she only knew.*

"Yes. Please note in the file that anything related to this search needs to be billed directly to me."

"No problem." Her tone is clipped as if I've offended her with my refusal to divulge any additional information. "When should we be expecting you back in Dallas?"

"Tomorrow." I don't mean to be short with my one-word answer, and it'll probably add to her irritation, but I want to get off the phone with her so I can text Cassie.

"Can't wait. I have a massive stack of reports waiting on your desk. Maybe we can go to lunch and go over them together."

"Sure. Sounds good. Talk to you tomorrow."

I might come off as an ass, but Becca's known me for years. She understands when I'm focused on something, there's no way of keeping my attention. She could be juggling bottles of Jack while hopping on one foot, and that still wouldn't keep me on the line.

Time to message Cassie.

ACTS OF SALVATION

REN: Hey. Got the results on the background check for you. Why don't you let me bring over some food tomorrow and we can go over them together.

I know. Ridiculous since there isn't anything to really go over, but that isn't going to stop me from capitalizing on an excuse to see her delicious curves in person.

CASSIE: Sounds good, but instead of you bringing food, why don't you let me cook for you... as a thank you for running the search.

Hell yes! The thought of coming home to Cassie cooking for me stirs up all sorts of primitive emotions, making me want to bang my chest and let the world know she's mine.

I quickly temper my emotions and reply as unaffected as possible, because there's no way I'm letting Cassie in on the fact that I'm over here grinning like a damned fool.

REN: Perfect. I'll be over at 7.

My fingers itch to add 'can't wait,' but I fear that letting her know how I truly feel will just make her run for the hills. If there's one thing I've learned about my little angel, it's that she's extremely skittish when it comes to emotions of the romantic variety.

Before I forget, I shoot Becca a quick email telling her to block off my evening. I typically work late on days when I'm in town, but that's definitely not happening while hanging out with Cassie is a viable option.

Before thinking too much of it, I quickly add in a request for a floral pickup, adding Cassie's information to the email. I know my little angel isn't into romance, but who wouldn't love fresh flowers in their space?

I shake my head, realizing I'm trying to justify buying flowers for a woman. This must be karma for all the one-night stands I've had over the years.

Whatever. Karma can shove it.

I'm getting Cassie the flowers, and if she refuses, I'll just have to make her see the error of her ways with more... persuasive measures.

As I type out the request, a flash of distant memories assaults me.

My father coming home with flowers for our mother.
Those same flowers ending up in the garbage later that
night. Our mother's tear-streaked face as she shut her
bedroom door without saying goodnight.

A lump in my throat forms and my chest begins to ache. I hadn't remembered that piece of my history in ages. To think that buying flowers for a pretty woman would stir up such dark memories leaves me with a ton of questions.

Are they really just flowers? And is she really just a pretty woman?

ACTS OF SALVATION

Cassie

Breathe, Cassie. *In... and... out.*

This is the first time I've had a man over to my place—like ever. And I'd be lying if I said I wasn't freaking out just a little. Okay, *a lot.*

Add to the anxiety that this man happens to be my best friend's uncle—and that we've had mind-blowing sex—well it's clear to see why I'm such a freaking train wreck right now. It's a miracle I haven't burned the place down with my absent-minded cooking!

I'm making filets with mushroom risotto and salad, as well as a tres leches cake for dessert. I know the steaks were spendy but I really want to impress him... *I mean, thank him.*

Besides, this is probably the kind of food he's used to eating. He's Bella's uncle, which means he comes from old money. Lord knows what he grew up eating. Certainly not reheated rice and beans on the daily, like me. It wasn't until my sisters and I got older that we were able to put in for groceries and expand our weekly menu.

Don't get me wrong, we had yummy food on special occasions, but I bet it still wasn't anywhere near what Ren is accustomed to.

Snap out of it, Cassie. Who cares what he's accustomed to! I shouldn't be trying to change myself or conform to some ideal just for a man. Regardless of how delicious he might be.

This is how it all starts... that dick-whipped slippery slope. It will be a cold day in hell before I let myself become a member of that club.

I lightly slap my cheeks, trying to snap myself out of this dick induced relapse. *Get. It. Together.*

Before I can finish my pep talk, there's a knock at the door.

There's no way out but through, so I head to the door and open it as casually as possible, praying he doesn't see the hot mess underneath.

"Cassie, you look stunning." Ren hands me a gorgeous bouquet of peonies in varying shades of pink.

The flowers are what's stunning, not me. I'm wearing distressed cutoff shorts and a black tank, nothing special.

I realize I've just been standing there staring at the flowers without saying a word, lost in my own head. Jumping into action, I quickly usher him in. "Where are my manners, please come in."

"I'm sorry if my compliment made you uncomfortable. I know we're just friends, but I couldn't help but point out how gorgeous you look. Bare. Without makeup."

I had every intention of not putting effort into my appearance tonight. I didn't want to make this feel like a date, and I somehow justified it by not getting ready for it. Pointless, I now realize. The way he's looking at me like he wants to devour me whole leaves no question that this isn't just a casual visit.

"You didn't make me feel uncomfortable at all. Just caught me off guard. This is what I always wear. What I always look like when I'm at home."

"Perfect." His voice is low and barely audible, but it tugs at something deep within me.

Choosing to ignore the feelings that single word evoked, I quickly change the subject. "So, I hope you like meat because I've made filets."

A look of frustration flashes across his eyes but he quickly schools it. "That's *perfect*."

There's that word again...

"Great. The meat is resting but it will be ready in a couple of minutes. Why don't I give you the grand tour?"

Ren gives me a salacious grin, punctuated with a wink. "By all means, please do."

"Oh, no. There will be no more magic happening between the two of us." I shake my head while placing my hands on my hips laughing.

His face turns serious as he gets to within an inch of my body, but not quite touching. "So you agree? It was magic."

My entire body flushes, and because I'm so fair, there's no sense in denying it. "Yes. It was magic. Very beautiful, hot, and delicious magic. But it could never happen again." The timer beeps, letting us know the steaks are done resting. Just in the nick of time.

"I guess that tour will have to wait." A smirk ghosts Ren's lips, and I can't help but feel that there's a double meaning to that statement.

But before I can ask, the sound of scratching has Ren's brows lifting and me running toward the noise—my bedroom door and where I've left Bruce.

"Should I be worried?" Ren's cautious gaze looks on from the living area.

"Maybe. I'm not sure yet. I've never had a man over to my place so I'm not sure how Bruce will react. Hold on one sec." I lift a finger as I slip through the bedroom door and away from his confused gaze.

Surely, a big bad alpha male such as himself won't be afraid of a large dog, right? I mean, he's one of the owners of WRATH, one of the best private security firms in the nation.

Scratching Bruce behind his ear, I give the verbal release for the command I've had him under. "Break." That one word has him up on all fours and sniffing at the door. "Good boy. That's mommy's good boy."

"Everything okay in there?" Ren's voice cuts through the door and I'm surprised Bruce isn't growling. Maybe things will go well after all. Grabbing hold of his harness, I walk my massive cane corso into the living area. "Ren, this is Bruce. Bruce, this is Ren."

"Wow, he's beautiful. May I?" Ren approaches cautiously with an outstretched hand, palm up and low to the ground. *Nice. He knows what he's doing.*

"So far so good. It looks like he might actually like you," I say, unable to hide the disbelief in my voice.

"Don't sound so shocked." Ren lets out a low chuckle, making Bruce lunge forward. I'm about to issue the command for stay when the unthinkable happens—Bruce begins licking Ren's palm.

Insane.

"You can close your mouth now. Dogs happen to love me." His warm smile melts me out of my stupor and into the present.

"They might, but Bruce is no ordinary dog. He hates anything with a cock. And you *most definitely have a cock.*" My entire face heats with the memory of his massive dick sliding in and out of me. *Ohhhh, how delicious that felt.*

Ren's nostrils flare and his breathing turns ragged, I guess he's just as affected by the memory as I am. Needing to break the sultry stare-off I bring up something that's sure to put a halt to both of our libidos.

"So... Bella was here the other day." *Yup.* My words have hit their intended target. "She told me about the vandal who attacked her car. Apparently they even shot out her tires. I mean, who does that?"

Ren stands from his crouched position and I don't miss the evident bulge in his pants. I guess bringing up his niece didn't completely douse out the flames of desire.

I motion us toward the table, determined to serve him the meal I cooked for us. Even if it's tepid by now.

Taking a seat at the small table, Ren speaks for the first time since my mention of his niece. "Yes, we still don't know who the perp is so we're taking every precautionary method possible. It's typically someone who is close to the inner circle or at least has easy access to it. Speaking of which, we should probably put some protection on you as well."

My fork halts on its way to my mouth, "Oh, hell no. There's no way I'm having a detail on me. I've seen what you guys are putting Bella through, and that's fine and all since she's the one who's been attacked, but I'm fine. I can take care of myself. Besides, I've got Bruce." I look to Ren's left where Bruce has stoically perched himself in hopes of getting scraps from his new bestie.

"Look, Cassie, I love your place but it isn't exactly in the best of neighborhoods. I'm assuming you walk Bruce at night, and he might be an awesome guard dog, but a dog can only do so much against an attacker or multiple attackers with a gun." He looks over to Bruce, patting him on the head. "I'm sorry, boy. I know you're fierce. I can see it in your eyes, but we have to do what's best for our girl, right?"

I shake my head and laugh. "Don't think I don't see what you're doing—buttering me up through my dog isn't going to work."

Ren shoots me a sly smile. "Okay, how about a compromise?"

"I'm listening..." I take a sip of the red wine I've poured for us both, watching Ren's cocked brow as he realizes what I've done. "What? It pairs perfectly with the steak, but I can drink yours if you don't want it." I reach for his glass but he's quicker than me, swiping it out of my grasp.

"Not so fast, little angel. I didn't say I didn't want it." He takes a purposeful sip of his wine before continuing. "Like I was saying, compromise. I'll be walking Bruce with you every night from now on." He looks up from his glass, begging me to argue.

"Okay." The word flies out before I have a chance to fully process what it means. I have no idea what possessed me to agree so readily, and by the look on Ren's face, he's just as surprised as I am.

"Okay," he echoes. That one word sealing the deal, and with it, whatever else it might bring.

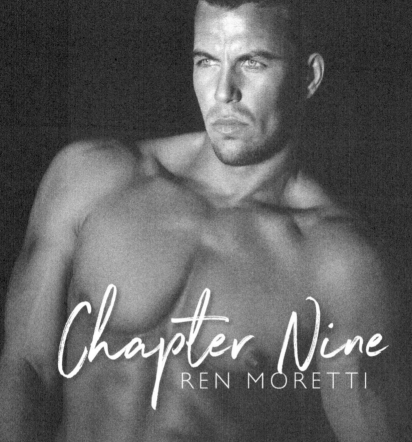

Chapter Nine
REN MORETTI

IT HASN'T BEEN A FULL twenty-four hours and I still have no clue what in the hell possessed me to offer myself up as a dog walking companion. With a full security company at my disposal, there's an endless supply of men that could do the job—but no, she wouldn't have agreed to just anybody and to be honest, nobody would be as vested in her safety as me.

Granted, someone else will have to watch her when I'm out of town, but whenever I'm in Dallas, it will most definitely be me.

I shake my head and chuckle to myself. Who'd of thought that I'd be so overprotective over a woman... other than my niece, of course. *My niece.* I cringe at that thought.

In all my years I've *never* expended energy on a woman other than a quick one-night stand. Not because I don't love them as a whole, but because they inevitably become complicated. *I don't do complicated.*

It takes up time and energy to deal with a woman's feelings. Time and energy that's better allotted in accomplishing more profitable or enjoyable things.

Until Cassie, I'd never met anyone who was worth deviating from that norm. It makes sense—in a totally sick and twisted way—that she would not only end up being a teenager, but my niece's best friend to boot.

Karma is one crazy bitch.

"What's that look for?" Aiden walks back into the main cabin of our private jet after taking a call in the bedroom. We're on our way to California for one of Aiden's clients.

I'm tagging along for the day to check over a security system, but I've made it clear I need to be back in Dallas by tonight.

Not only do I have my dog walking date with Cassie, but I also have a meeting with the Renzetti *Famiglia*, and someone named Johnny DeLucci.

"Come on. Spill it," Aiden prods. "I've never seen you this tense. You're usually the carefree one in our motley crew of dysfunctional men."

How do I tell my brother what's up without divulging who it's about? I proceed cautiously. "It's about a girl."

Aiden lets out a roll of laughter while slapping his knees repeatedly. "Ohhhhh, the eternal bachelor has fallen! I thought William was full of shit, but now I see that it's true."

ACTS OF SALVATION

Note to self, kick William's ass for talking about me behind my back. Even if it was just good-natured ribbing, he should have known better than to go to my brother with that bit of conspiracy theory.

I roll my eyes and shake my head. "Go on. Let it all out."

"Come on, now. You know I'm just teasing. I'm happy for you, *fratellino*." Aiden wipes at his eyes. Glad to see that I've made him laugh so hard, he's cried. "It's about damn time a woman got through that thick armor of yours. You know not all women are like our mother, right?"

His words give me pause. Could that be the reason behind my never settling down? Nah.

"If anyone had any part in my bachelor ways, it was our father. After Mom, he never brought another woman home. Sure, he had his fair share of fun—something I'd rather not think about in detail—but if he instilled anything in us it's that women were an inconvenience for anything other than fucking."

Aiden shakes his head in disgust. "Please don't tell me you really think that, Ren. You have a niece, is she only good for one thing?" He raises a brow in warning, letting me know to tread carefully.

"Of course I don't think that. Obviously some women out there are worth their weight in gold, but more often than not you end up with women who are more trouble than they're worth. Finding one who is truly special is like bagging a unicorn and I didn't want to spend time looking when odds were I'd end up with a gremlin instead of a majestic creature."

"Did you just compare women to gremlins?" Aiden sucks in his lips, trying to contain his laughter.

"Not all. Just most."

"So, this woman that's got you tied up... she must be a unicorn then."

Visions of Cassie flit around in my head. "Oh yeah, she's majestic alright."

"Well, you know how rare those are. I say hang on to her and don't let go. No matter what." He reaches across, patting me on the shoulder. "And like I said before, she isn't Mom. If she's as magical as you say she is, she won't just leave you after you've given her your heart."

And therein lies the truth. My fear of abandonment has been the catalyst to every action in my adult life that revolved around women. If I kept them at a distance, never truly giving myself away, then they couldn't hurt me when they inevitably disappeared from my life.

I look out the small window, clutching my tumbler of Jack so tightly I feel the skin around my knuckles tighten.

"Hey. Don't close up on me, fratellino. All I'm saying is that maybe this one is worth taking the risk." He leans back into his seat, pulling up his phone and giving me a reprieve from his words.

But the problem is that the silence is worse. It leaves me alone with my thoughts. Thoughts of Cassie and the fact that she is one hundred percent worth the risk. Thoughts of how she's already refused me time and time again, but despite that, I know that I'll be diving headfirst into those hazel eyes.

That woman is mine. Come hell or high water.

ACTS OF SALVATION

I'm about to lift my hand to knock on Cassie's door when I notice that it's been left open. Immediately this sends up red flags since this isn't the type of neighborhood where people do that. Cassie wouldn't be so reckless, *would she*?

Multiple possibilities assault me all at once, the most prominent one being that the same attacker who targeted Bella is now here—for Cassie.

Adrenaline pumps through me as I unholster my weapon of choice, a Springfield XDM Compact. Keeping it low to the ground, I enter the apartment cautiously. Everything is quiet. No sign of a scuffle or Bruce for that matter.

Shit, did Bruce get out during the attack?

Nails clicking on concrete have me spinning around at full speed, and what I see makes my breath halt.

Cassie. In a sports bra and running shorts. So. Much. Bare. Skin.

"Are you insane?!" Cassie hisses at me while trying to keep Bruce from jumping up and licking my face.

"Are *you* insane?!" I wave my hand up and down, pointing out the getup she has on. "You're wearing *that* in *this* neighborhood, all by yourself... *at night*. Are you asking for trouble?"

"I'm not by myself. I have Bruce and this." She moves one of her hands to her keychain, retrieving a tube of pepper spray.

I let out an exasperated breath. "Cassie, a little tube of pepper spray isn't going to do you much good if you get attacked from behind, or if the attacker has a gun." I step closer, bringing her into my arms. "I'm sorry if I come off as overbearing, but you had me worried sick. I saw the door open and thought someone had taken you."

Cassie's body stiffens, causing me to drop an instinctive kiss to her temple in an attempt to soothe her.

"I guess I must've left the door open when I left to walk Bruce." She mumbles against my chest. "It won't happen again."

"Why didn't you wait for me? I told you I'd walk Bruce with you." I bring both of my hands to Cassie's waist, squeezing enough to make her look up at me. She feels so good in my arms—fitting like the perfect puzzle, complete with that feeling of fulfillment after having located the missing pieces.

"I didn't think you were serious. Besides, I can take care of myself." My spicy little angel has so much fire.

Let's see if she can handle a little heat.

Shutting the door with one hand and spinning her around with the other, I catch her by surprise. Taking advantage of the moment, I push her up against the door and whisper into her ear. "What would you do if someone attacked you from behind, just like this... pinned you to the wall, just like this."

She bucks her ass against me, letting out a searing hiss when it brushes against my growing erection.

Running a splayed hand up her bare torso, I revel in the goose bumps my touch leaves behind. As I inch my hand upward, Cassie's breath turns ragged, the anticipation of what's to come driving us both mad.

Once I've reached my destination, I work my hand underneath the hemline of her sports bra, cupping one of her very full breasts. *God, how I love them.*

A low growl escapes me as my palm brushes against her erect nipple. The flesh soft and warm under my grasp. So feminine and real.

"What would you do, my little angel, if someone touched you like this..." I let my other hand travel south, all while Cassie pants heavily, letting me know she's just as aroused as I am. Lifting the hem of her shorts, I bury my hand lower, finding the silken folds that confirm my suspicion.

She's wet.

Taking my middle finger, I run it along her drenched slit as she moans. "Ren?"

I halt my movement, "Yes, baby?"

"Don't stop."

I smile against the skin of her neck, giving it a quick bite as I thrust two fingers into her wanting pussy. Cassie throws her head back, letting out a moan of satisfaction as she grinds herself onto my hand.

My baby knows what she wants and she isn't afraid to take it. *I fucking love it.*

"Sooo...." Cassie mewls, "close."

Already? She must be as hot and bothered for me as I am for her. God knows I'm about to spill, and all I'm getting is a contact high.

I continue to thrust my fingers in and out as I angle the pads, hitting her sweet spot. Lifting my other hand up to her throat, I lightly squeeze, bringing her face to mine. Our eyes lock and those hazel eyes pierce my soul, saying a million things at once and yet nothing at all.

My chest constricts, and I feel suffocated by a tidal wave of emotion. Our eyes flicker back and forth, leaving no question that she feels this overwhelming sensation too.

Wanting to silence the thoughts racing through my mind, I

plant a possessive kiss on her perfect mouth.

Biting her lower lip before sucking it between my teeth seems to be her undoing. Cassie lets out a moan as she begins to contract, pulsating around my fingers as she comes down from her high.

Fuck if that wasn't the most intense sexual experience of my life. Not even our night at The Pearl came close to this.

"That was... intense," Cassie murmurs as she slides out of my grasp, instantly making me feel the loss.

"Yes. I think it proves that what we have is special." I bring my hand up to Cassie's face, brushing the pad of my thumb against her cheekbone.

"I think that what it proves is that this"—she motions between us—"is dangerous. And it can't happen again. I mean it, Ren." She schools her face, hiding any trace of emotion. "This was a lapse in judgment. Nothing more."

Her words are like daggers to my chest. If I weren't up against the wall already, I would've physically stumbled back.

I clench my jaw before nodding once in agreement. "If that is what you want, then that is what you'll have."

My phone vibrates in my pocket. Looking down at the number, I see that it's from New York. *The Renzettis.*

"Gotta run. I'll be here tomorrow for our walk." Opening the door, I look back one last time and issue her a warning. "*Don't* leave without me."

I shut the door quickly, not giving her the chance to respond. It seems my little angel is in need of a *time-out.*

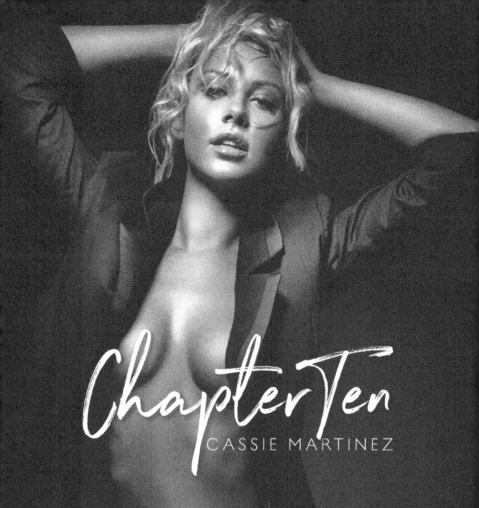

Chapter Ten
CASSIE MARTINEZ

THINGS HAVE BEEN GOING wonderfully. *Wonderfully platonic.*

It's been weeks since the incident with Ren, and true to his word, he meets me himself or sends one of his men to help me walk Bruce every night.

Also true to his word, he's given me exactly what I've asked for. A strictly platonic relationship.

I'm not going to lie, I've felt like an idiot on multiple occasions for having shoved him away that night. But then life happens and after every relapse, I'm reminded of *why* we're such a bad idea.

The main one happens to be walking next to me this very moment.

"So, are you going to tell me why you're sulking? We're surrounded by Chanel and Prada. Nobody should be sad around Chanel and Prada. It's sacrilegious, especially to a fashionista like you." Bella grills me with her stare, and I know she won't stop her inquisition until she gets what she wants. *Information.*

"Okay. I'll tell you if you tell me what's going on with you and William first..." I place the ball in her court, sure she's going to buckle and change the subject.

I'm wrong.

"Ugh! That man is infuriating. One minute he's hot, the next he's cold. I don't know which side is up with him." She stops walking and pulls me into one of our favorite bistros in Highland Park Village.

Immediately, the maitre d' spots us and heads over.

"Ladies! How lovely to see you again. Shall I seat you at your regular table?" The gorgeous brunette with raven eyes motions us to the right.

"Yes, please." Bella smiles warmly at her before stepping in tow.

We're seated in the courtyard overlooking a beautiful fountain, which you'd think would soothe my nerves—but it doesn't.

Maybe Bella's forgotten our conversation?

"Like I was saying..."

Not a chance.

"William is hot one minute and cold the next. Did I tell you his ex showed up at the house demanding to see Harper? I mean, the woman abandoned her one-year-old daughter and comes waltzing in months later as if it were no big deal!" The busboy places a carafe of water on the table before pouring us both a glass. "They have a meeting with their lawyers soon and I'd be lying if I said I wasn't nervous. What if the judge gives Harper back to that crazy woman?"

"I'm so sorry, Bella! I had no idea all that was going on." A brick of guilt sits in the pit of my stomach. Here I am obsessing over the status of my relationship with Ren—*her uncle*—when she herself doesn't know whether her man's daughter is being taken away from them.

Now is *definitely* not the right time to come clean about my indiscretions.

"Oh, girl. Don't worry about it. I hadn't really told anyone because even I'm not sure of what's going on between William and me. He has enough on his plate with his crazy ex. I don't want to be something else he has to worry about."

Before I can say anything, my phone starts vibrating on the table. Quickly snatching it up, I slide the messaging app open—praying Bella didn't see who the sender was.

REN: Your place in two hours.

That's two hours earlier than usual. *What if I had other plans?* I roll my eyes, something that doesn't go unnoticed by Bella.

"Who was that? And why did you snatch up your phone like it was the last golden ticket?" Bella's slanted brow lets me know I can't sidestep out of this one. *But maybe I can do the shuffle.*

"Some asshole I've been *not* seeing." I take a sip of water, needing the liquid to quench my suddenly dry mouth. "He gave me the cold shoulder after a heated night and is just now texting me for the first time in weeks. Seriously, he's not worth the mention."

Not *totally* a lie. This technically is the first time he's texted me since the incident that shall not be mentioned. And so what if I'm the reason for the cold shoulder.

"What a jerk. Don't give him another thought." Bella lets out a noise of disgust before flagging down our waiter.

It's time to up the ante on our beverage situation.

I'm stumbling to the door of my apartment, realizing we probably shouldn't have ordered that extra round of drinks. Oh well. *C'est la vie.*

"You're late." Ren's deep voice has me raising my gaze, coming face-to-face with the chiseled embodiment of perfection.

Nope, I totally made the right call with that extra round.

I ignore his jab at my tardiness as I try to open the front door, all while reminding myself that pushing him away was the right thing to do. I repeat it over and over in my head like a mantra.

Off-limits, off-limits, off-limits.

"What's off-limits?" Ren's puzzled expression lets me know I was thinking out loud.

Well, fuck. Time for some damage control.

"What? I didn't say anything." I greet Bruce before continuing toward the loft's kitchen, away from his scrutinizing gaze. "Any news on the stalker front? Is it safe to drop our guard now?"

"There's been some news, but we still need to get everything confirmed before we can let everyone else know." Ren looks away, avoiding my eyes. *Interesting.*

"Are you not sharing because you think I'll tell Bella?"

Immediately Ren begins to pace. I've definitely hit a nerve but I'm not sure if it's because of Bella being my best friend, or if he really thinks I'd tell her something he'd share with me in confidence.

His phone goes off, killing any chance I have of asking any follow-up questions.

"Hey, Becca. Is everything ready for tonight?" Ren, who was a ball of anxiety moments ago, is now donning the biggest smile known to mankind. Seriously, it's something that belongs in the book of Guinness World Records.

I open and shut my utensil drawer a little too loudly. *Who is this Becca, and why does she make Ren so fucking happy?*

Ren chuckles, and I'm not sure if it's at my blatantly petty behavior or something Becca said.

"Can't wait. Thanks, babe."

Both brows shoot up to my hairline. *Babe*? Well, I guess he hasn't been wallowing like I have.

"So, what were we talking about?" The corner of Ren's mouth lifts into a smirk.

"This Becca must have some sort of hold on you if she made you forget Bella's would-be attacker." I purse my lips and give him the side-eye.

"Must..." Ren is outright full-bellied laughing now. "As for the attacker. We're still keeping our guard up. Just because they've been silent, doesn't mean they aren't planning their next attack."

ELEANOR ALDRICK

I turn away from him and open the refrigerator door, unable to let him see how much he affects me. I rummage through its contents, unsure of what I'm looking for, but knowing the cool air is at least helping the red in my face disappear.

I know he doesn't owe me any explanations when it comes to this Becca, but fuck does it still burn.

"Surely you could at least let up on having a detail on me every night. Bella is the target, not me." I finally turn to face him holding the milk carton before placing it on the counter.

His face is impassive, not giving anything away. "About that... we need to talk." Ren's eyes narrow as he steps around the granite island, coming mere inches from where I'm standing. "We've been seeing each other a lot lately..."

Not sure where he's going with this, but it's making me nervous. I quickly open the takeout containers I brought home, waiving the contents in Ren's face. "Cheesecake? It's the best in town."

"I'm good thanks."

Damn. It's bad if he's refusing food. The man is the equivalent of a human garbage disposal.

"I don't think we should let up on having someone walk with you at night, but I do think maybe I should step back a little."

My chest. There's a hole in it. That's the only reason that could explain this soul-sucking pain I'm feeling right now.

He must guess his words have affected me because he tries to soften his blow. "You can still call me if you need anything, Cassie. You know that, right?"

"Uh-huh. Yup. Got it." I touch the tip of my tongue to my top lip and slowly nod once before biting the lower lip.

ACTS OF SALVATION

I will not cry. I will not cry. My treacherous eyes begin to tingle, unwilling to listen to what my brain is telling them. I need to shut this shit down now.

"And no worries. There's no need for me to call you. I've been taking care of myself long before you came along. If I need something, I'm sure I could make it happen on my own."

"Cassie, stop. You're being ridiculous. I'm not saying I don't want to be your friend anymore, I'm just saying I think it's for the best if someone else takes my post during your walks with Bruce."

Oh hell, no he didn't. Did he just call me ridiculous?

"I think it's time for you to leave. I need to walk Bruce, and before you say anything, it's still broad daylight and the streets are packed with people. There's no need for you or anyone else to accompany me." I walk over to the door and swing it open, leaving no room for interpretation. He's worn out his welcome.

Ren shakes his head as he begins to walk out. With every step he takes, my heart splinters and cracks, taking the remnants with him.

He stops outside the threshold, and with his back to me, issues the killing blow. "Goodbye, Cassie."

I slam the door, sliding down against it, finally releasing the silent tears I wouldn't shed before him. Closing my eyes, all I hear are the echoes of his words, burning down whatever shards of my heart he's left behind.

Goodbye.
Goodbye.
Goodbye.

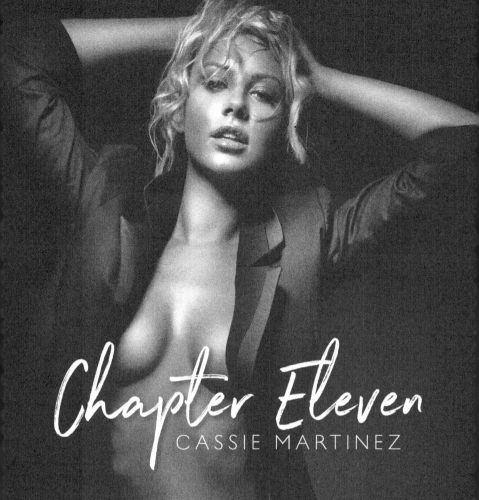

Chapter Eleven
CASSIE MARTINEZ

"REALLY, CASSIE. I DON'T see what the problem is." Blair takes a giant swig of chardonnay before continuing her plea. "Can't you simply drop off my husband's tux on your way home? He's leaving straight for the gala from his office."

No, Blair. Nothing is simple when it comes to your husband, Creepy McCreeperson. But of course, I don't say that.

I'm the only one left who can pay Mom's bills. My sister Aria got laid off, Carmen's husband got injured at work, and Ceci is hiking through Budapest trying to find herself. I'm not even going to mention my brother's whereabouts. *Like father, like son.*

"Yes, of course, Blair. It's no problem at all."

"Fantastic. By the way, I'm so glad you came around and decided to sign the contract with us."

"Me too." *Like I had a choice.* I plaster on a fake-ass smile and hand her the new pair of Manolo Blahnik I ordered, being careful not to drool all over them.

Blair catches my lingering gaze and gives me a smirk. "You best get going now, don't want you to get stuck in traffic. The gala will start soon and Woodrow can't be late."

Oh, yes. Because Turtle Creek is known for its bumper to bumper traffic of Bentleys, Rolls Royce, and G-Wagons. I internally roll my eyes.

"Of course, just text me if you think of anything else you might need." Giving Blair a tight smile, I pick up my purse and shuffle to my impending doom.

"Cassie! So good to see you again, and so soon. What a treat!" Barbie's extremely cheerful demeanor is going to send me into a diabetic coma if she doesn't tone it down a notch.

"Hi, Barbie." I offer her a warm smile, it isn't her fault she's all rainbows and sunshine. "I've brought Dr. Wilson his tux for the gala tonight."

"Wonderful! I'll let the doctor know you're here." Her high

ACTS OF SALVATION

ponytail bobs repeatedly with her nods as she dials McCreeperson's extension. "Yes, I have Ms. Martinez here to see you... uh, okay." She looks up from her desk, blinding me with another megawatt smile. "He asked that you please head straight to his office. No need to knock."

"Okay then." I nod once as I pass her, trying not to show my growing sense of alarm. I'm not exactly thrilled to be in close quarters with the good doctor. Our last encounter left much to be desired.

Wanting to get this over with as quickly as possible, I push open the door and step into Creeperson's office.

Aaaaaand, I'm immediately blinded by what stands before me. *McCreeperson in nothing but his boxers. His very tented boxers.*

"I'm so sorry. Barbie told me to head straight in without knocking." I spit out my words a mile a minute as I whirl around to face the wall. I don't need to stare at the man's junk any longer than necessary.

I hear shuffling before I feel his presence behind me. "No need to apologize. I'm sure you've seen plenty of boxers in your line of work."

I shoot out my hand, loosely gripping the hanger containing his tux with my fingers, waving it around like a madwoman. "*Here* is your tux for the evening, Dr. Wilson. Please let me know once you've dressed."

After a couple of beats of silence, I begin to hear the rustling of fabric, and finally, a zipper being opened then closed. "All done, Ms. Martinez. You may turn around now."

I whirl with the fury of an F5 tornado and begin to lay into McCreeperson. "I'm not sure what kind of personal stylists you've worked with before, but let me assure you that I have never—not once—in my entire career as a personal shopper seen a man in his boxers. Let alone, one who seems to be visibly aroused. If you would like for me to continue to work with your family, let this be the last time you make an insinuation of that nature again."

"It wasn't my intention to upset you, Cassie. I thought surely you've assisted a man with measurements before and therefore seen him in his skivvies. And as far as being aroused, that's just my normal state. I'm a shower, *not* a grower." The man has the balls to punctuate that with a wink.

I shudder in disgust while reminding myself of Mom and the money she so desperately needs. "If that'll be all, I have to get going."

I'm about to place my hand on the doorknob when McCreeperson speaks up. "Actually, could you assist me with this bow tie? I've never been good at getting these things on."

"Of course, not a problem." I begrudgingly set down my bag and stand on tiptoe to help the man with his tie. At five-two I won't be walking the runway anytime soon.

"You know, Blair and I have an agreement."

Lord, please don't let this be going where I think it is...

"Our marriage is one of sheer convenience, you know." His eyes narrow as he pierces me with his sleazy stare.

I'm about to shoot off another snarky remark when the door swings open. *Thank god for Barbie.* "Dr. Wilson, your car service is here."

I mouth a silent thank you to Barbie, unsure if she knew what she walked into, but wanting to cover my bases just in case.

"Wonderful. Thank you, Barbie." McCreeperson places a hand

on my shoulder, squeezing it before quickly releasing it. "Goodnight Ms. Martinez. It was lovely seeing you again."

I turn away, unable to look the man in the eye and simply nod. That's when I notice Barbie scurrying off as if she were on fire. *God, I hope she doesn't think I was getting all cozy with the McCreepster.* I make a mental note to clear the air with her at some point. But for now, all I want to do is go home, bust out the vodka and watch re-runs of *Desperate Housewives*—my guilty pleasure.

Home. Sweet. Home.

I'm about to kick my feet up on my couch when there's a knock at the door. That's odd, I wasn't expecting anyone. I quickly grab my trusty tube of pepper spray and it instantly reminds me of Ren.

Fucking Ren.

Since I live in an older warehouse conversion, our doors don't come equipped with a peephole, making the first step in my security system a good ol' fashioned holler.

Bellowing into the door, I ask, "Who is it?"

"Me, now open the door. I come bearing gifts!" Bella's welcomed voice seeps through the cracks of the old metal door.

Quickly opening it, I find my best friend does indeed bring gifts. Bella holds up a large takeout bag from Renzetti's, our favorite Italian joint.

Renzetti's. Ugh. That also reminds me of Ren and how he

wanted to take me there on the first night we met.

"What's that face for? Not in the mood for Italian?" Bella's brows drop in confusion as she makes her way toward my kitchen.

"No, that sounds perfect actually. If you hadn't brought food, my dinner would have consisted of olives and vodka."

Bruce lets out a snort of disapproval as he plops down on his doggy bed. I angle my head toward him and cock a brow, "Don't you judge me, Bruce. At least I'm not the one eating straight out of a garbage can."

Bella lets out a laugh. "Oh, man. He's still doing that?"

"Yes, it's his favorite pastime right along with butt-sniffing." I pull the utensils out of the drawer before taking a couple of cartons to the coffee table where we end up eating most of our meals. "So, what brings you to my hood? Don't get me wrong, I'm definitely not complaining and you're always welcome. I'm just curious."

After a beat of silence, I finally look up from the takeout box I've pried open and see Bella looking down at her lap, refusing to look me in the eye. "*Uh oh.* Spill the beans."

"I don't think I want to go to college in the fall."

"Oh, god. Is that it? I thought you were going to tell me you got a VD from Mr. Wonderful!" I'm laughing so hard I have to put the container down for fear of spilling the pasta all over the floor. "Girl, that is *not* a big deal. I started working at Louvier's when I was sixteen as an inventory clerk and eventually worked my way up to what I am today—a glamourous personal stylist with a six-figure salary to boot." I roll my eyes, clearly indicating my sarcasm because this current gig is anything but glamorous. "No, but in all honesty. Do what you love and the rest will follow. If I've learned anything in my short life, it's that life isn't always guaranteed and that you need to make the most of it while you can."

"You're right, I know. But it's still terrifying. I had my entire life mapped out and to think that it could all turn out so different... Anyway, I just needed some time with my bestie. Take my mind off of college, William, and his psycho ex. Tell me more about this oh so glamorous job of yours. Is McCreepster still giving you problems?"

"Yes! You will not believe what he did today." I tell Bella about the latest shenanigans Dr. Wilson pulled, and it's enough to make her whiskey shoot out of her nose.

"Oh, that burns! That burns!" Bella shrieks.

I quickly hand her a stack of napkins with one hand while wiping away a tear of laughter with the other. "I'm sorry. I should have issued a warning with that story."

"You owe me for that." Bella shoots me a playful glare. "I honestly can't believe the man had the balls to do that to you! Has he no decorum?"

"None. The man doesn't even care that, to him, I have a boyfriend named Bruce."

Bella snorts, bringing one hand to her belly and the other up, making the universal sign to stop. "Nooo, you told him Bruce was your boyfriend?"

"Yup. And that still wasn't enough to stop his advances. If only I had a real boyfriend, then maybe what's-his-face would actually back the fuck off."

Bella chokes on her eggplant parm as my words sink in. "I'm sorry, did I hear you correctly? Did Cassandra Marie Martinez, the eternal bachelorette who's patented the ban on love just say she wanted a *boyfriend*?"

"Yes, Bella. You can lower your brows now." I roll my eyes as I shake my head. "They're going to permanently affix themselves to your hairline if you don't drop that look of surprise."

Bella snickers. "I'm sorry. I don't mean to tease, it's just I never thought I'd hear those words come out of your mouth... It's the dawn of a new era, I guess."

A new era indeed.

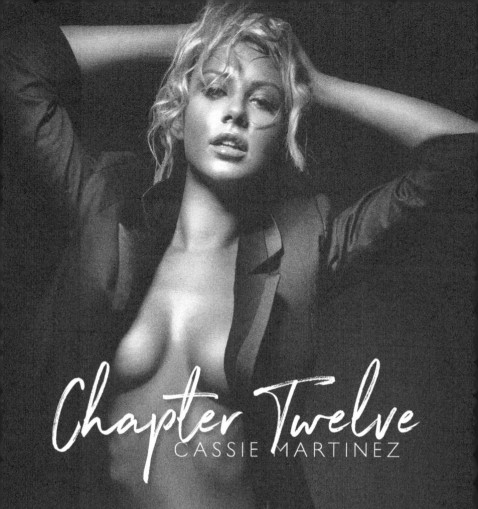

Chapter Twelve
CASSIE MARTINEZ

I T'S BEEN A WHIRLWIND COUPLE of weeks. The only good thing that's happened as of late is the fact that Dr. McCreepster went on his yearly mission trip, performing reconstructive surgery on children with cleft palates in South America. *Maybe he isn't so bad...*

In any event, his trip means that there haven't been any additional tent sightings and I've been able to collect my pay without drama.

The same could not be said for poor Bella. Her dad was shot while on the job and is now in a coma. I know that life-threatening injuries are a very real possibility when working at a private security firm, but the reality of it actually happening is still shocking.

And to add insult to injury, not long after, William dropped her ass like a sack of potatoes and went back to his psychotic ex.

Fucking men. The root of all evil if you ask me.

Anyway, this is why I find myself outside of Bella's California home, waiting for her to answer the damn door. She and her twin brothers are staying here while her father is being cared for at a local hospital, which is good, but I'd be lying if I said I didn't miss her.

After five minutes of waiting, I decide it's time to make a call.

The line rings, and rings, and rings...

"Woman! It's about time you picked up your phone. Open your damn door, already."

"What? Why? Are you here?" Bella sounds as confused as my *abuelita* with her remote.

"Yes, bi-atch. And I just cleared the million security guards you have surrounding the house, so let me in."

Bella opens the door, squealing in delight at the goodies I've brought for her. I'm holding up a bottle of tequila in one hand and a pint of ice cream in the other.

"Oh my god, Cassie! How did you get here?!"

I step across the threshold, thrusting my gifts into her hands before embracing her in a bear hug. "An airplane. A little birdie told me you were moping around here like some pathetic excuse of a woman. And *that* my friend, is unacceptable."

It's true. William's sister, Ashley, called me after picking up Harper last week. Said Bella was a sorry sight, so clearly I had to come to the rescue. That's what besties are for.

"What, I'm not allowed to grieve the loss of a man—A man

who I thought was the love of my life?"

Bella's words have me whirling around like the Tasmanian devil. "First of all, that man was not the love of your life. The love of your life wouldn't just abandon you like that for some psycho bitch who is a *terrible* mother." I wave a finger in the air while pursing my lips. "Second of all, no. You are not allowed to grieve that piece of shit garbage of a man."

"Okay. So what do you propose I do then?" she asks, a small smile lifting at the corners of her mouth.

"You put your badass woman panties on and put yourself out there again. Literally. Go put on your sexiest panties and meet me out here in thirty. I'll watch the boys while you get ready for dinner. I made the four of us reservations at this new restaurant in Malibu right on the water." I open my arms wide, spanning an imaginary oceanfront view. "The fresh air will do you good and it's about damn time you do something outside of the house besides visiting the hospital."

We've made it to the kitchen and it's absolutely gorgeous. It's coastal chic, with white marble countertops, and a sea glass backsplash that is simply stunning.

Bella lets out a long breath of air before shoving the ice cream into the massive stainless-steel freezer. "Okay. You're right." She turns and begins walking out of the kitchen, "I'll be ready in thirty. Make yourself at home. If you need anything while I'm in the shower, just ask the boys. They're in the media room at the end of this hall."

"Okay, take your time. That hair is going to need all the help it can get. When's the last time you washed it?" I bellow after her, partly joking, partly not.

"Ha. Ha. I get it. I'm a hot mess." She disappears into a room, leaving me to my own devices.

Cocktail time it is.

We've made it to the restaurant, managing to snag a table in their open patio overlooking the surf. The smell of the salt water is refreshing compared to landlocked Dallas and I can't help but smile.

"I loooove Malibu! So many fun places to eat." The pre-dinner cocktails have lifted my mood and my tone ends up resembling something similar to that of Barbie's. *Note to self, switch to water.*

Rightfully so, Bella shoots me a death glare. "I know you're trying to help, but could you tone down the happiness just a bit. It's making me want to strangle you, and we can't have that. Who will care for the boys if I'm locked away on murder charges."

"Well, that escalated quickly," I murmur, shooting the boys a side glance as they giggle. For two seven-year-olds, they're pretty sharp.

"I know. Sorry. Couldn't help it." Bella squeezes her eyes shut as she takes a sip of her drink.

Poor girl. She's in bad shape. I need to do something to snap her out of this funk, STAT.

"I met someone." I blurt out before thinking things through. Sure, by 'met someone' I mean casually flirt, but she doesn't need to know the specifics.

ACTS OF SALVATION

"Oh my god, Cassie! That's amazing!" Her cheerful face tells me I've done something right, even if it is bending the truth slightly. Bella reaches for my hand, squeezing it in a death grip. "Tell me everything."

"I'm not telling you this to rub it in your face, Bella. I swear there's a point to this conversation." I purse my lips, scrunching them to the side as I try to figure out what in the hell I'm going to say. "A while ago, I met a man who I thought could be the one. Things were progressing rather quickly and then all of a sudden he dropped me like a sack of potatoes, leaving me destroyed."

That much is true. She just doesn't know that this man is her uncle.

"How in the hell did I not know about this?" Bella shoves at my shoulder in disbelief.

"You had a lot of stuff going on. I didn't want to add to your worries. Anyway, the point is I didn't let myself wallow. I got right back on the horse and ended up meeting an amazing guy." Again, I use the term 'met' loosely.

The gentleman in question is my Krav Maga instructor who I've been seeing the past couple of weeks. My paltry tube of pepper spray left a lot to be desired, so I signed up for a course at a local gym. Lucky for me the instructor happened to be a hottie with a penchant for vertically challenged women.

He'd been asking if I wanted to join him and his buddies for drinks after class but I'd shot him down every time. But I think Bella's sorry state is deserving of an outing.

I shoot Bella a mischievous smile. "I think it's time for all of us to hang out. What do you say? Want to meet my new beau and his bestie?"

Bella squints at me, her eyes narrowing into thin slits. "Are you trying to set me up and disguise it as a meeting with your new boyfriend?"

"Who me? I would never. I just thought you wouldn't want to feel like a third wheel is all."

"Uh huh. Sure you didn't," Bella says sarcastically. "As tempting as your offer might sound, I think I'll have to pass. I'm definitely not ready to put myself out there again. Now if you'll watch the boys for me, I have to go to the ladies' room."

"Okay, but we're resuming this as soon as you get back."

She might think she's done with this conversation but it's far from over. "She thinks she's got it all figured out, doesn't she boys?"

Both boys snicker before going back to their private conversation—something having to do with Minecraft.

A buzzing sound draws my attention. Looking around, I see that Bella's napkin is vibrating on the table. Removing the piece of cloth I see she's left her phone out.

Picking it up, I'm able to see who the caller is. The picture that lights up the screen is that of her uncle, Ren—instantly causing me to panic and drop it back on the table as if this were a game of hot potato.

The phone stops vibrating but resumes its taunting two seconds later. By this point, the boys have caught wind that something's up. Like something straight out of *The Shining*, they both look up at me in unison and demand for me to answer the phone already.

Figuring it must be something important since he's dialed back to back, I hit answer before I lose my nerve, "Hello?"

"Hello... Cassie?" Ren's masculine voice elicits a visceral reaction, causing me to visibly shudder.

"Yes, this is she. Bella stepped away for a second. Can I help you with something?" It takes everything in me to keep my voice calm when internally I'm about as freaked out as a priest at a wet T-shirt contest.

There's a long pause and I'm not sure if Ren's hung up or he's just as shocked to be on the phone with me as I am him.

"Ren, you still there?"

"Um, yes. Yeah, I'm still here." There's fumbling on the other end of the line before he continues. "I was calling to let Bella know that Aiden is awake. Can you please let her know that she and the boys are needed at the hospital as soon as possible?"

His words shut down all other emotional faculties, and all I'm able to feel is rainbows and sunshine. "That's amazing!" I blurt into the phone while bringing a hand to my heart. "I'll let her know as soon as she gets back to the table."

"Thank you, Cassie. Take care." The line goes dead and I'm once again brought back to the reality of our situation and how awkward it is.

Screw it. With news like we just received, there's no room for sadness. It's time to celebrate and be merry.

Cin cin, motherfucker.

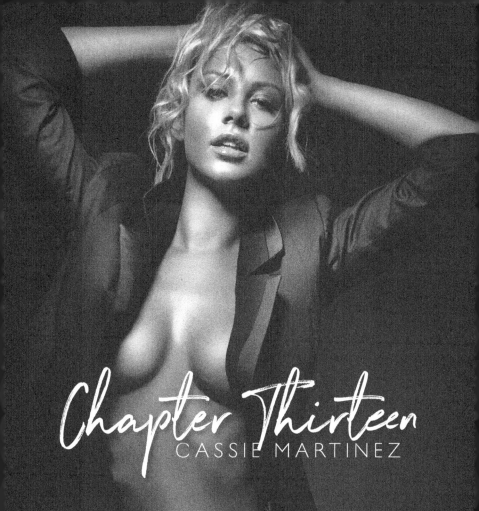

Chapter Thirteen
CASSIE MARTINEZ

WELL, MY CHEERSING WAS a bit premature. An hour later and we all find ourselves in the hospital waiting room. My cheerful mood all but a distant memory as I stand next to Ren's deliciously ripped body.

Trying to focus on what he's saying is extremely difficult. All my mind wants to think about is how his lips have traced the curve of my nape or how his hands roamed my body not too long ago.

Bella pokes my side, shooting me a curious glance. *Oops, I guess I was staring.* "You okay?" she whispers into my ear. "You don't have to go in with us if you don't want to. I didn't ask you how all this would make you feel."

"Don't be silly, Bella. Your father is awake after a massive brain injury. I will be here in whatever capacity you need me to be."

Bella pulls me in for a hug, squeezing the remaining air out of my lungs. When I look up, Ren is staring at us with brows furrowed, making my stomach do all sorts of backflips and somersaults.

William, who'd showed up at the restaurant in Malibu to try and win Bella back, nudges Ren in the shoulder. "You were saying, man?"

"Apparently, only five people are allowed in the room at one given time. We'll be going in two groups. The first shift of visitors will be Bella, the twins, Cassie and myself."

My heart squeezes at the fact that he's included me along with his family. *Get a grip, Cassie. It's probably just because of your relationship with Bella.*

William comes up behind Bella and squeezes her shoulders in an attempt to comfort her. I'm not sure the rest of the group is aware of the relationship they have, or how Ren would feel about his niece hooking up with his best friend—especially since that friend recently broke his niece's heart.

I don't know what excuse he offered as an apology for his behavior, but the two seem to be amicable as of right now. If I were Bella, I'd make William sweat it out a bit longer, make him pay for his sins.

Everyone taking the first shift begins to shuffle out of the waiting area and into the hall. Before entering Aiden's room, Ren turns around and issues a warning, "Remember what the doctor said, no shocking information that could mess with his recovery."

We all offer a nod in agreement as he opens the door and we all step inside. Bella's dad is laying in the hospital bed staring at the ceiling but as soon as we come in his entire face lights up.

"My family," he whispers.

Immediately the boys run to their father, enveloping him in an embrace. The sight brings tears to my eyes. Not only did the twins lose their mother, but they came very close to losing their dad too.

A hand caresses my face, wiping a tear away. Startled, I look to my left and see Ren has been watching me.

A myriad of emotions assaults me all at once. The tenderness in his eyes is so contrary to the aloofness he's offered me the past couple of weeks and I'm left a puddle of confusion.

"Cassie, would you mind taking the boys out for some fresh air. I'm sure they're tired of seeing their dad in a hospital bed." Aiden's voice cuts through my fog.

A whole conversation transpired during my internal struggle, and I'm just glad I was able to catch the tail end where I was being addressed.

Luckily the boys cut in, giving me a chance to pull myself together. "Nooooo," they wail. "We want to stay here with you!"

"I have to talk to your uncle and sister about grown-up stuff right now, but I promise we'll be home soon and you can spend as much time with me as you want. So much time, you're going to get sick of seeing me." Bella's father strokes their heads in affection.

The twins finally relent and follow me out the door as Bella mouths me a silent thank you. *No, Bella, thank you.* I needed to get out of that room and clear my head before I combusted from the overload of emotion.

Going from not having seen Ren in weeks to being mere inches from him, his affectionate hands caressing my face, trying to bring me comfort—it was all too much and remaining in that room one second longer would have proven to be disastrous.

Ren

"Don't." I shut William up with one word because I'm really not in the mood.

We're on our way to Bella's California home, trying to hunt her down after she disappeared from the hospital.

It doesn't take a genius to figure out these two have had some sort of lovers quarrel. After having found out about his relationship with my eighteen-year-old niece, things have been strained between the two of us.

I'm nowhere near being okay with this information, but the fact that I myself am lusting after my niece's nineteen-year-old friend does soften the blow a little. Can't exactly hate my best friend for being in an extremely similar situation to what I'm dealing with myself.

He, however, has no inclination of what's been going on with me and Cassie though—and I plan on keeping it that way. At least until I've come to terms with whatever he has going on with Bella.

We pull up to the home and I haven't even completely rolled to a full stop before William is flinging himself out of the car like a bat out of hell.

"Whoa there, buddy. We already have one man in the hospital, don't need two."

"I need to talk to Bella." William's wild eyes let me know he has some serious making up to do, and I definitely don't want to know the details.

The front door swings open and a flustered Cassie stands before us. "It's about time someone showed up. I have a flight to catch and I haven't been able to get a hold of Bella."

"You're leaving tonight?" William's cheerful tone is so at odds with the situation that it leaves me wondering what plan this man has up his sleeve.

"I wasn't supposed to but I got a call from my employer saying she needed me tomorrow morning for a charity function. Seeing as how she's my sole source of income, I think it's best if I keep her happy. Don't you?"

"Yes. Totally understandable. Why don't you let me take the boys from you and you can catch a flight back with Ren? He has to be back in Dallas for a job as well."

Cassie chews on her bottom lip, no doubt thinking if avoiding a flight with me is worth losing her job over.

"I don't know... let me check with the boys and see how they feel about staying with you until Bella gets back. Granted, I know y'all were all living together as of last week, but a lot has happened since then." Cassie lifts a brow and shakes her head, clearly displaying her disapproval of William's latest shenanigans.

With a sigh, Cassie disappears down the hallway, no doubt on her way to the media room where the boys are probably located.

Turning toward William, I give him the side-eye. "You really think she'll be okay leaving the boys with you? And before you answer, no, I don't want to know whatever it is you did to my niece. I don't want to have to beat the shit out of you."

William lets out a nervous chuckle. "God, I hope so. It's my last

ELEANOR ALDRICK

Hail Mary at intercepting Bella today. Just know that when you're in love, you will stop at nothing and that includes offering free child care and a free ride on a private jet. Besides, I've missed the boys. It's been over a week since I've schooled them on some Mario Kart."

I hope he's right. Not because I want him making up with Bella but because this would give Cassie and I an opportunity to be alone for a couple of hours. We definitely need to clear the air after the whole mishap at her apartment.

As if summoned by my thoughts, the fiery beauty appears before us. "Okay, I've talked to Matt and Max and they are in agreement, providing you supply them with pizza for dinner. And no, Auntie Cassie has no objections to them having ice cream for dessert. I brought some over earlier today when I thought we'd be having a girls' night in."

I'm not gonna lie, the words 'Auntie Cassie' have me feeling all kinds of possessive, and it scares the shit out of me. I know she's been dubbed auntie because of her closeness with Bella but I can't help but imagine it as stemming from her being mine.

And *that* right there is why the fuck I've stayed away. The deeper I got caught up in all that was Cassie the more I was inundated with consuming thoughts of *always* and *forever*—sending up all sorts of red flags to abort mission and run the other way, especially with her pushing me away at every turn.

"Deal. That's definitely doable. Do you need any help packing? Can I get you something for your trip?" William's overly eager tone doesn't go unnoticed by Cassie, and she isn't having any of it.

"Down boy. Save all that sucking up for Bella. From the looks of things, you're going to need all the help you can get." She pulls her phone out, rolling her eyes while shaking her head. "It looks like my flight just started to board, so if it's okay with you, Ren, I'll be catching a ride with you back to Dallas."

Her piercing hazel eyes stare icicles right through my soul, chilling me to the bone. When Cassie is happy, her gaze is like the morning sun, warming and all enveloping—but when she's pissed, you might as well have taken a polar dip in the deep arctic.

"No problem at all, Cassie. I'd love to have your company on the flight home."

She forces out a puff of air through her nose, all while keeping the same impassive face. "Right, well I'll be ready in fifteen minutes. I take it you'll wait for me then?"

I suck in my lips, trying to fight the smile her tough chick act is pulling out of me. "Of course, Cassie. Wouldn't dream of leaving without you."

William squints his eyes, looking back and forth between us. "Do I even want to know?" The bastard has the audacity to shoot me a smirk.

"Not unless you want to have that heart-to-heart about my niece..." I raise a brow, challenging him to press me on this.

Just as I suspected, William's lips press into a thin line as he crosses his arms over his chest, giving me the universal sign of back the fuck off.

"Uh-huh, that's what I thought."

ELEANOR ALDRICK

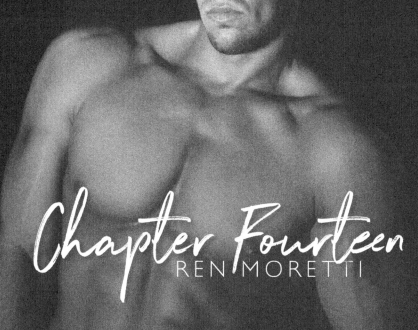

Chapter Fourteen
REN MORETTI

"C**ASSIE, YOU'VE IGNORED ME** the entire trip home." Things have gone from humorous to frustrating. The woman is completely ignoring me despite being seated right next to me.

One of the perks of flying private is not having nosy nellies butting into your conversations. The flight attendant even gave us a wide berth, no doubt noting the palpable tension between Cassie and I. But still, the maddening woman didn't spare me a single word.

Having landed ten minutes ago, we're now in my G-Wagon on

our way to Cassie's and it's my mission to get her to talk to me before then.

"Why are you acting this way?" I attempt reaching out to her one more time, thinking maybe if I make her see she's acting like a child she will see the error of her ways.

Apparently not, all it does is earn me a glare. Hell, that's more than I've gotten thus far so maybe I'm onto something.

"You're acting like a child. I have no idea what I've done to earn this cold shoulder."

Ding. Ding. Ding. I've hit the jackpot. Cassie's face turns a pretty impressive shade of red before she opens her mouth and unleashes her hellfire.

"You haven't done anything wrong. I'm simply giving you the space you require."

My brows squeeze together. "What? What are you going on about? Is this because I haven't been by to walk Bruce? Does my little angel miss me?"

I bite the edge of my lip, knowing I'm poking the dragon at this point.

"No. Of course not. I don't need you to walk Bruce with me. I'm more than capable of handling myself."

"I think we proved that theory wrong with my little demonstration, didn't we?" Visions of me fingering Cassie up against her door have my cock hardening almost instantly. A low guttural sound escapes me, the need to have her again consuming me completely.

"That was a mistake, and the only reason you were able to pin me was because I let you." My little angel has her claws out, ready to play.

"How about we have a repeat. See if you can prove me wrong." I can't help it, the corner of my mouth lifts in a mischievous smirk.

"We're here. Thank you for the ride, both the flight and the ride home. I can see myself in." The little spitfire hops out of the car before I can stop her.

Quickly following her lead, I get out of the car, grabbing hold of her bag and refusing to let her carry the duffel up to her loft by herself. "This thing weighs a ton, what'd you pack? Your entire wardrobe?"

"Ha ha. Very funny. I didn't know how long I'd be staying or what we'd be doing. Besides, nobody asked you to carry my bag." Cassie picks up speed, apparently trying to get our little quality time over with as soon as possible.

"Where's Bruce? Will I get to see him tonight?" I know I'm stalling the inevitable, but if playing twenty-one questions will buy me some extra time with Cassie then so be it.

"He's with my mom, and no, you will not get to see him tonight or any other night."

We're almost to her door but I can't take one step further with her being so damn pissed at me. I grab hold of her arm and bring her into my chest. "Stop. I don't know why you're so mad at me but I'm sorry. I'm sorry if I hurt your feelings, it wasn't my—" the door to her apartment pulls my attention, making me stop mid-sentence.

There are visible marks around the wood trim by the doorknob—clear signs that someone's been tampering with the lock. Quickly moving Cassie behind me, I go into full protective mode. "I need you to go back to the car and call Titus, tell him we need a crew over at your place, ASAP."

I hand her my phone, unlocking the contacts, but she isn't

having any of it.

"No. Why don't *you* go to the car and call them?" She places her hands on her tiny waist as if to say she isn't going anywhere.

Oh my little angel, how you try me.

Picking her up by the waist, I throw her over my shoulder and carry her to my SUV, ignoring her small fists to my lower back. Once she's safely inside with my phone, I lock it from the outside.

I point to the phone, "Call Titus. Now."

She might be pissed as fuck, but this is for her own safety and I won't play nice just to appease her when there's a real possibility some psycho is still in her apartment, waiting to hurt her.

I step away from my car, knowing that's the safest place for her to be. The windows are bulletproof and I'm the only one who can unlock it. Short of a bazooka, nothing can touch her.

Back at her door, it is blatantly obvious someone either tried or was successful in breaking in. There's only one way to find out.

I withdraw my weapon from its holster, keeping it low to the ground I kick the door open, wanting the element of surprise in case someone is still here.

The smell of shit hits me like a bat to the head. It's everywhere. Smeared all over the walls, dragged across the floor, and rubbed all over Cassie's furniture.

Someone wanted to make a statement.

"Holy shit!" Titus chuckles while pulling the collar of his T-shirt over his nose. "No pun intended."

"Now isn't the time for jokes, asshat. Can't you see someone is trying to fuck with my girl? And how'd you get here so fast?"

"I was at a bar down the street when your little firecracker called." He bares his teeth, sucking in a sharp breath. "About that, I passed her on the way in and she does not look pleased."

I raise a hand, spanning it across the open living area à la Vanna White. "She refused to cooperate. Please tell me you'd do something differently given the circumstances?" I cock a brow, knowing full well Titus is as alpha male as it gets. I wouldn't be surprised if he was into that BDSM shit, making his women bend to his beck and call.

He lets out a low laugh, almost a snicker. "No, I wouldn't, but my women are very different than the little wild one you're now calling your girl. Does Bella know?"

Shit. I hadn't realized I'd let that slip.

"No. And I'd appreciate it if we kept it that way." Scanning the room, I see a photograph pinned under a particularly fresh pile of shit.

Upon closer inspection, I see that it's a picture of Cassie. Well, Cassie with her eyes scratched out.

"Wow, that's twisted."

"You can say that again. I need you to call a team in, have them check for prints or any other information they're able to gather."

"Got it, brother. I'll also call our cleaning crew. A lot of this stuff needs to be tossed. Hope Cassie doesn't mind rebuilding her pad from scratch."

"Oh she's not coming back here, ever."

Titus brings a hand to his mouth, holding back a snicker while shaking his head. "Another one bites the dust."

"What? She'd be safer at my place." Both of my brows drop, unsure of what the big deal is.

"Right. Because she couldn't go stay at William's. That place is locked up tighter than Fort Knox."

"William isn't here, he's in California. And besides, he's already got his hands full with Harper and Bella. Not to mention his sister is also staying there."

Titus' expression shifts ever so slightly at the mention of Ashley, William's sister. To the untrained eye, it would seem that Titus is unaffected, but to me, it's glaringly obvious. "So, Ashely?"

"Drop it, brother." Titus takes on a no-nonsense tone. For someone who's been all jokes tonight, his change in demeanor is extremely enlightening.

Knowing not to push when he's like this, I acquiesce and drop it... for the most part. "No problem. I'm here if you want to talk, though."

"Got it, Dr. Phil. Why don't you take your lady back to your pad. I've got everything handled here. Should we find anything, you'll be the first I call." Titus brings a hand to my shoulder, patting it a couple of times before he walks toward the far end of the loft, clearly exceeding his brotherly bonding for the night.

"Sounds good." I walk out, leaving him behind to deal with his own demons. It's time for me to deal with my own—a little hellion named Cassie.

Stepping into the G-Wagon, I notice she's just as fired up as when I left her. "I'm surprised the windows aren't fogged up with all the smoke coming out of your ears, little angel."

I chuckle as Cassie flings the cell phone at my face.

"So, can I go in now?" Her pouty lips are glistening, begging me to bite them. I love it when she's all fired up like this.

"No—"

Before I can finish my sentence, Cassie's hands fly to the door handle. Unfortunately for her, she isn't quick enough and I've managed to hit the lock feature before she can open it.

"Listen, little angel. I swear there's a good reason."

"You have five seconds to explain before I start screaming bloody murder."

"Shit."

"*Shit?*" Cassie's face scrunches together and I swear I've never seen a more adorable sight.

"Yes. It's smeared all over your apartment. The floors, walls, furniture, and even the ceiling in some parts."

Her face morphs from angry to scared. It stirs something in me, a need to keep her safe, making sure she never fears anything ever again.

"Don't worry, baby. You're coming home with me. We'll figure out who did this, and more importantly, we'll make them pay."

My words have their intended effect, she softens, melting back into the seat.

Thank god she isn't fighting me on this one. I really don't feel like having the firm's attorney battle a kidnapping charge, and that's exactly what I'd have to resort to had she not agreed.

But to keep her safe, it'd totally be worth it.

"Who would do that?" she whispers into the night.

"A dead man, that's who." I grab hold of her small hand, giving it a firm squeeze. "I'll keep you safe, Cass. I promise. All you have to do is let me."

She finally gifts me with a small smile, bringing light into this dark night. "Okay. I promise I'll try."

"Good. Let's take you home."

And if I were being completely honest with myself, I'd know that this is the moment I truly fucked myself over. Bringing Cassie home would make her that very thing.

My home.

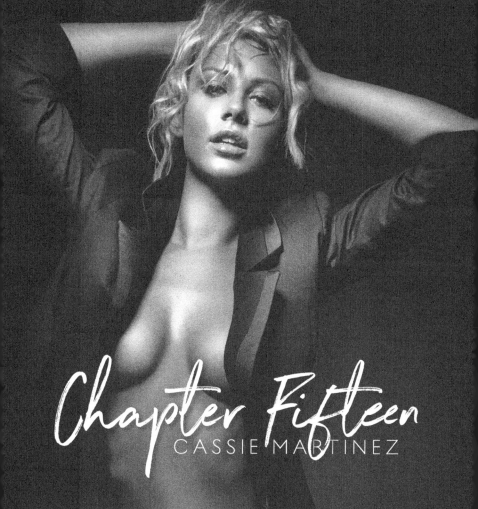

Chapter Fifteen
CASSIE MARTINEZ

I T'S THE MORNING AFTER the literal shit show at my apartment. My whole body shudders at the memory of it all. Who in their right mind would take the time to do something so disgusting?

Whoever did it is clearly disturbed. That's one of the main reasons I didn't fight Ren when he suggested we come back to his place last night. I didn't want to stay in a place where a psycho had been. Besides, I could only imagine what my loft smelled like.

"What's the face for, breakfast not to your liking?" Ren smiles up at me from his coffee mug. He's wearing nothing but gray loose-fitting lounge pants, his taut abs on full display and ready to be licked. I'd like to have *him* for breakfast...

Focus Cassie, you're still mad at him.

It's six in the morning and Ren has already managed to put out a spread of bagels, assorted cream cheese, and fruit. My stomach grumbles in protest, remembering I didn't get a chance to eat dinner last night. "No, it's wonderful, thank you. You really didn't have to. I could have grabbed something on my way to the gym."

"You can work out here. I'm not letting you out of my sight." Ren's tone leaves no room for argument, but that doesn't stop me.

"Excuse me? I have a ton of things to do today. You can't just follow me around all day like a personal bodyguard."

"Fuck if I can't. Someone trashed your place, Cassie. Do I need to remind you of that?"

He has a point. Whoever did that to my place isn't just going to disappear because I've changed locations.

Feeling defeated, I sit my ass down on a kitchen stool, letting my forearms rest on the cool granite surface of the island. "Suit yourself, but we're still going to my gym. I leave in ten minutes."

Didn't think it was this kind of gym, did you buddy? Strolling up to the Krav Maga studio, I can feel Ren's questioning gaze but I'm not willing to let him in on the details just yet.

As soon as we step through the double doors, I feel at peace.

ACTS OF SALVATION

The one thing I'll forever be grateful for is the sense of empowerment these classes have brought me.

"Hey, beautiful." Mateo greets me from the other side of the large room. Immediately, I feel Ren's body bristle beside me. *Oh, this is going to be fun.*

"Hey, handsome." I shoot him a wink before pointing toward Ren. "Sorry about the entourage today. Had an incident last night and I'm saddled with a bodyguard for the day."

Mateo's facial features go from playful to all business in two seconds flat. "Who do I need to fuck up, babe? Just say the word and their ass is mine."

Ren cuts me off before I even have a chance to answer. "That won't be necessary. Her man's got it covered. The name is Ren." He extends his hand in greeting, and Mateo takes it but I don't miss the questioning glances he throws my way.

I claim temporary insanity, but I decide to let Ren's claim on me slip. I sort of like this possessive side to him. It's a lot better than the aloof one he'd been feeding me the past couple of weeks.

Besides, the man is going to suffer heavily watching me grapple with this Italian stud for the next hour or so. The least I could do is refrain from busting his balls for the rest of the session.

As predicted, Ren's facial expressions throughout my session with Matteo left nothing to the imagination. The man was not pleased.

Sure enough, as soon as we step back into his SUV, Ren has something to say. "That's the last time you'll be training there. I can have one of the instructors with the firm work with you. They can even come up to our place, that way you don't have to trek back into Deep Ellum for this."

Our place. The label doesn't go unnoticed, and I can't say that I hate how it sounds.

Never in a million years did I think that I'd even be contemplating living with a man, but Ren somehow makes it all okay. Every moment spent with him feels like home. We connect without having to utter a single word, anticipating each other's needs before they've even arrived. The only thing holding us back is me and my damn fear of control.

It's all too much too fast... *though that walk-in closet of his might help soften the blow.*

Ren's place is gorgeous. It's the penthouse in one of the most prestigious buildings downtown—there's even a doorman and everything.

Shuddering at the thought of what his monthly payment is, I decide I will not be offering to go halfsies.

"Now where to?" Ren's question pulls me from my mental tangents.

"So is this our new norm? You following me around to all my appointments?" Surely this man has better things to do than to be my shadow all day.

"Until we get more information on who trashed your place last night, yes." Ren keeps his eyes on the road, not giving any indication that he's joking.

"Okay, well then I guess to my mom's. Ready to meet the family?" I tease, sure that he's about to turn the car around, but to my surprise, he maintains the course.

"Good, it's about time I met the woman behind the force that is my little angel." Ren shoots me a wink, before getting on I-75.

Noticing he's heading toward Oak Cliff, I can't help but blurt, "How do you know where my mom lives?"

"I pulled your info last night after the attack. I'm not taking any chances, Cass. I need to know everything about you if we're going to catch whoever did this." His tone is serious, and I can feel the undercurrent of concern so I drop it. "While we're at it, any other Matteo types I need to know about? Anyone is a possible suspect at this point."

I scoff, "It wasn't Matteo. And no. You pretty much already know anyone in my small circle aside from my family and the Wilson family."

"The creepy husband still giving you problems?" Ren's face contorts into a murderous stare.

"It couldn't have been him. He's in South America, performing reconstructive surgery on little kids." After a beat, I add, "Maybe I was wrong about him."

"Cassie, always listen to your gut. That could give him a plausible alibi, but I'll look into it. We could never be too sure."

Ren pulls up to my moms, and I'm sure the neighbors are rubbernecking all the way down the block. I don't blame them. A G-Wagon in this neighborhood is typically nothing but trouble.

"Cassandra?" Mom's small frame shows up behind the screen of the front door.

"*Si, Mama,*" I say as I remove myself from the exquisite Italian leather covering the seats of Ren's car.

Ren quickly walks around the car, opening the door the rest of the way before closing it behind me. *Who knew he was such a gentleman?*

"And who is this fine man you've brought home?" Mom's eyes rove over Ren and I can't help but blush at her perusal. *Holy hell, Ma!*

"*Limpiate la baba,*" I whisper under my breath, telling my mom to wipe her drool.

Ren beams at my words and I'm left wondering if he understood what I said. *God, I hope not.*

"It's a pleasure to meet you, ma'am. It's clear to see where Cassie gets her beauty from."

Mom preens at Ren's high praise. "Oh, I like him, *mija.*"

"He can hear you, Mom." I roll my eyes as I make my way to the back yard where no doubt Bruce is lounging. "I take it my man is back here?"

Before I can open the back door, Ren puts his hands on my waist, pulling my back to his chest and whispering into my ear, "That title belongs to me and me alone, little angel."

My breath stutters as I feel the length of his arousal brush against my ass. No words. The man leaves me with no words.

Ren chuckles as he walks around me, opening the back door and greeting Bruce as if he hadn't just rocked me to my core.

I'm about to step outside and join them when Mom grabs my arm, effectively keeping me in the kitchen.

"Is it serious? It's the first guy you bring home, so it must be serious, right *mija?*" Mom pulls out her old-as-hell address book and starts flipping through the pages. "Should I call the church now?

They book out a year in advance, you know..."

Jesus take the wheel, this woman is out of control.

"No, Ma. This is all very new, so I'd appreciate it if you kept the wedding plans to zero."

Mom shoots me a doubtful look. "You know that man looks at you like you're his next breath, right? That, paired with the fact that he's the first man you bring home, a mother could only assume wedding bells aren't too far off."

"I get it, Mom. I promise you'll be the first to know if anything in our situation changes."

"Like the fact that you've moved in with me?" Ren's wicked grin appears through the door, bringing along a traitorous Bruce with him. I swear my dog might love Ren more than he loves me. I've never seen him so taken with anyone as he is with Ren.

Turning toward mom, I see that her jaw has just about hit the floor. Oh yea, Ren just revealed our living situation. One that I haven't even fully come to terms with.

"It's not permanent, Mom. I'm having some work done at my place and I'm staying with Ren until it all gets worked out." There's no way I'm telling my mom what really happened. She already has a lot to worry about without having to add a psychopath to the mix.

Ren walks up behind me, wrapping me up in his big strong arms. "We'll see about that. I think the best place for you to be is with me, permanently."

"*Dios mio*. This man knows what he wants!" Mother fans herself as she conspicuously slides me her address book, causing me to roll my eyes. "Shall I fix you both something to eat?"

"Maybe next time, Mom. We still need to get Bruce situated in his new surroundings and then I have a meeting with the Wilson family for a charity luncheon they're putting together."

"Okay, but next time you come over don't forget to bring that handsome man of yours."

Ren, who is still holding on to me, chuckles into my hair. "I wouldn't dream of letting her forget."

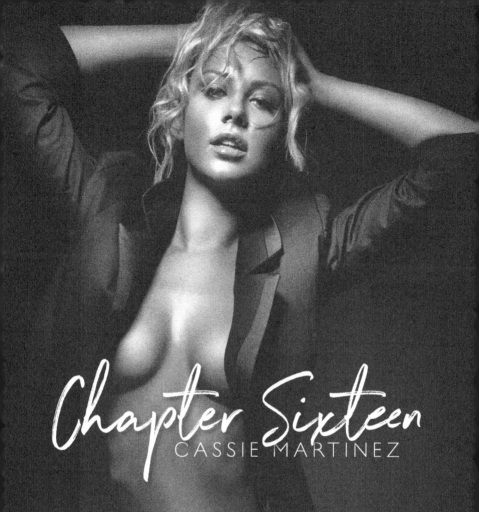

Chapter Sixteen
CASSIE MARTINEZ

I *REALLY* LIKE REN'S PLACE. Not only does the penthouse have everything I could ever want from a home, it's also conveniently located across the street from a dog park smack dab in the middle of the city. Perfect for Bruce.

Speaking of the devil, the shameless beast took to Ren's apartment like a fish to water. We had to pry him from the massive U-shaped sectional and I don't blame him one bit, the seats are extra deep and the cushions are filled with down feathers, making you feel like you're sinking into a cloud every time you lay on them.

We finally managed to entice him with a walk and now find

ourselves at the beautifully maintained dog park. Finding a bench, Ren and I plop down as we watch Bruce mingle with a gorgeous white boxer.

"Looks like someone's found himself a girlfriend." I chuckle.

Ren clears his throat and that's when I notice the tall brunette attached to the white boxer, beelining it for our bench.

As soon as she's within earshot she begins talking at full speed, "Ren, is everything okay? I didn't hear from you last night. I've been worried sick."

My head spins at what her words could imply. Who is this woman and where'd she come from?

"Becca." Ren's one word clues me in on all I need to know. It's Becca. The woman who can make him smile as wide as the Grand Canyon. "I'm sorry I didn't call. Just a heads-up, I'll be out of touch for the next couple of weeks."

The brunette turns to me, glaring, before beginning a tirade in Spanish. "*Y esta güera? Es ella la razon? Tu nunca traes tus conquistas a la casa.*" And this blond, is she the reason? You never bring your conquests home.

I let out a slow sarcastic laugh. This bitch thinks I don't know what she's saying.

My parents are from Guadalajara, Mexico, where a great portion of its citizens are of European descendants. I might not look like the average Hispanic with my hazel eyes and fair skin, but Spanish is my first language and she's got another thing coming if she thinks I'm just going to let her rude-ass behavior slide.

My blood turns into molten lava, bubbling and ready to boil over. I stand my full five-two, staring her straight in the eyes before I let her have it, "This *güera* is most definitely the reason, and of course he brought me home. It would be sort of difficult not to seeing as how I now live there too."

My words have their desired effect. As Becca stumbles back in surprise, I seize my opportunity and flee the scene. I'm positively fuming, and I couldn't care less that I've left Ren behind to deal with the fallout of my words.

Snapping Bruce's leash on, I exit the dog park and leave the shitty encounter behind.

I've just reached the penthouse elevator when I feel him.

"Why'd you leave like that, Cass? You know we need to have eyes on you at all times. That wasn't smart."

"I know you didn't just call me stupid." I don't turn around to face him, I can't. I'm still angry, and if I were being honest, a little jealous. The private elevator opens and I step inside, knowing he'll follow.

"Dammit, Cassie. Quit twisting my words. All I'm saying is that you can't just run off like that. It isn't safe." I chance a quick glance at him, noticing he's really mad. Oh well, that makes two of us.

"Excuse me for not wanting to interrupt a reunion between you and *Becca*." Her name rolls off my tongue like a day-old piece of rotting fish.

His laughter startles me into looking up. The man is bowled over, hands on his sides, laughing his ass off. After a good minute he finally stops, straightening himself as the elevator door opens and we both step out.

Whirling around in the entryway, I shove him with one finger. "What is so damn funny?"

Ren wipes at a tear. "You are. You are what's so damn funny. I can't believe you're jealous of Becca. She's like my little sister and also happens to be my secretary."

Okaaaay. So that could potentially explain why she was worried—if he didn't check in for a job. "Do you normally call her at night? She said she was expecting you to reach out to her last night."

Ren shoots me a devastating smile as he unleashes Bruce and pulls me into his arms. "Yes. I normally handle work around the clock when I'm in town. One of the perks of being an owner. We're always on duty." He places a kiss on my forehead. "But I'm sure a certain someone could persuade me to change my ways every now and again."

Ren is one of the five men of WRATH, all co-owners of the nationwide private security firm. It makes sense that he'd check in with his secretary. It's all part and parcel of running your own business, but that doesn't mean that I have to like it. Or that I have to like her.

"What's going on in that pretty head of yours?" Ren strokes my hair as he looks down at me through lust-filled eyes.

"What're we doing, Ren?" I'm not one to put labels on things so quickly but everything has been moving at light speed since last night and I need to do something to protect my heart. It almost shattered completely the last time he walked out on me, and we weren't even officially together.

His face goes from hungry to lost in a matter of seconds, letting me know he's just as confused as I am.

"I don't know, little angel. All I know is that this feels right and that I don't want you anywhere else. Can't that be enough for now?" His eyes are pleading, but I'm not sure I'm willing to give myself away for a sliver of hope at something real.

"I don't know… I guess we can try taking it one day at a time." I push my lips to the side, unsure of what I've agreed to. Hoping to God that whatever it is, it doesn't end up breaking me in two.

"So this is where the McCreepster works." Ren's words are more of a statement than a question.

Blair sent us up to Dr. Wilson's practice in order to pick up a check for her charity luncheon. Apparently McCreeperson is the one with the purse strings in the relationship and I don't blame him one bit. With the way Blair spends money, she's liable to run them to the ground on her chardonnay habit alone.

We enter the overtly gaudy waiting room and I could tell Ren's thinking the same thing I did when I first laid eyes on this place.

Lowering himself to my level, Ren whispers into my ear, "Ostentatious much?"

"Behave." I snicker while giving him a playful shove.

"Cassie!" Barbie's greeting is as warm and friendly as usual.

"Hi, Barbie. This is Ren, Ren, this is Barbie, 's nurse."

"Pleasure to meet you." Ren extends his hand in greeting and Barbie is all too happy to take it.

"Right, well now that introductions are done, do you mind calling the doctor and letting him know we're here to pick up a check?"

"He's been expecting you so feel free to go on back." Barbie's eyes flicker back and forth between Ren and I. "Would you mind if I borrowed your gentleman for a minute? I need to pull a couple of boxes down from the utility closet and Dr. Wilson isn't able to help for fear of injuring his hands."

I roll my eyes. Of course, Dr. McCreeperson would be too good to help with manual labor. "If it's okay with Ren, it's okay with me."

I can tell he wants to follow me instead, but ever the gentleman, he concedes. "Sure, no problem. Lead the way, Barbie." Before he disappears in the opposite direction, he looks back toward me, "Give me a holler if you need anything, okay?"

I love that he's always thinking of my safety. It makes me feel like he truly cares, and I'm not just some favor because of my relationship with his niece.

Bella. Shit, I need to catch her up on everything that's been going on. I wonder if she's back in Dallas yet. Ren mentioned she'd be coming home as soon as they released her dad.

Reaching the good ol' doctor's door, I'm sure to knock. Definitely not wanting a repeat of the tenting incident.

"Come in," Dr. Wilson's voice booms from the other side of the door.

I'm glad to find him fully clothed and a good distance away. "Hi, I'm here to pick up the check for the luncheon. Blair said you'd have it ready for us."

"Us?" He rounds his desk and heads toward a chest of drawers by the door... by me. Pulling out a large binder, I begin to relax a little.

Stop freaking out, Cass. That's just where he keeps his checks.

"Um, yes. I'm here with Ren," I say casually, hoping he'll infer that he's my new boyfriend even though the mention of Bruce did nothing to stop his advances last time.

Placing the binder on top of the chest of drawers, Woodrow walks the space between us, stopping only once he's a mere inch from me. Lifting a hand to my chin, he begins to slowly run the pad of his thumb across my lips. "Please tell me he's not your boyfriend, beautiful? It would break my heart."

The door flings open, and it takes a moment for me to gather my bearings. Finally breaking free of the twilight I'm in, I turn to see Barbie standing at the threshold, mouth agape. But it's the site behind her that really has my stomach churning.

It's Ren, and his face is the perfect depiction of silent fury. His jaw is clenched, the grinding of his teeth glaringly audible. And his eyes, I've never seen such fire in his eyes. I'm afraid of what he might do to McCreeperson if I don't step into action now.

"Dr. Wilson, like I was telling you, this is Ren—my boyfriend. Now if you'd please be so kind as to write the check so we could be on our way, we'd greatly appreciate it."

Dr. McCreeperson takes his time in picking up the binder and writing the check. He's about to hand me the damn thing when he halts his movement midair, making a point to stare straight at Ren before speaking, "Let me know if there's anything else I can do for you, Cassie. I'm sure that I can give you *anything* you need."

Ah, hell no. Why couldn't he just keep his mouth shut.

Sure enough, Ren walks straight toward him, snapping the check from his grasp. "Thank you for the check, but if I ever catch you placing one of those greedy little hands on my woman again, I can assure you that lifting boxes will be the least of their concern."

A mental image of Ren taking a hammer to Dr. Wilson's hands flashes before me and I shudder. There's no doubt in my mind that he'd carry out that threat without qualms.

"Come on, Rambo." I tug at Ren's shoulder, offering an apologetic smile to Barbie on our way out.

Finally outside the building, I try deflection. "Did you see the look on Barbie's face? Poor thing had no idea what kind of creep she'd been working for. I bet she'll be looking for a new job as soon as possible." I offer Ren an awkward chuckle but he isn't buying any of it.

"Speaking of looking for new jobs, how about you leave that one and go work for someone else?"

"Ugh, I was afraid you were going to say that. It isn't that easy when it comes to finding clients who are in need of a personal stylist. You need networking and connections, neither of which I have. Besides, I'm pretty sure that contract I signed is ironclad."

"Don't worry about the connections. William's sister, Ashley, can set up some meetings for you. As for the contract, let me have the firm's attorney look it over. He lives for that stuff."

"Really? Oh my god, that would be amazing!" I'm so excited I don't mind my surroundings, jumping up on the man and climbing him like a tree before peppering his face with kisses.

Ren grabs my ass and squeezes. "Oh, I can get used to this."

Me too, handsome. Me too.

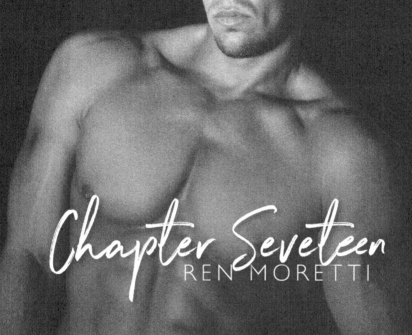

Chapter Seveteen
REN MORETTI

I F SHE KEEPS KISSING me like this, I'm liable to fuck her right here in the damn parking lot.

It's been absolute torture having her prancing around me all day, tempting me with her sweet curves and fiery temper. Making me want to bite that wicked mouth of hers.

And that's just what I do. Taking her bottom lip into my mouth, I suck on it hard before biting down. "Shall we take this home, baby girl?"

"Mmmhhhm," Cassie moans into my mouth as she grinds her warm cunt on my abs.

"I need to get you in the car before we're slapped with indecency charges."

She laughs as she slides off of me, sashaying to the other side of the car. "Don't act like it wouldn't be worth it."

And that right there is the problem. For her, I'd endure anything, give up everything, and become anything she fucking needed me to be. The power she holds is unprecedented, and it scares the shit out of me.

"Everything okay?" Cassie's eyes search mine, but I'm not giving up that secret so readily. She might hold a massive amount of power, but she doesn't hold all the cards. I need to keep an ace in my pocket.

"Yes. Just need to get you home as soon as possible before my dick breaks off from how hard it is." I look at her out of the corner of my eye, and sure enough, the woman is smirking. "Uh-huh, you know what you do to me."

"Why don't we take care of that now?" Cassie reaches over the center console, unbuckling my belt as I pull onto the street.

I know we should probably wait—we're in midday traffic and if another SUV were to look into our car, they'd get a show—but fuck it, I need her like a crack addict needs his next hit.

Cassie pulls me out, causing my cock to jerk in her small fist and making me groan.

"Well someone's excited to say hello," she purrs as she lowers her mouth to my glistening tip. This woman doesn't waste any time with taunting licks or amateur kisses. No, my woman takes me in, all at once and without mercy.

Fuuuuuuck. My foot presses on the gas pedal, needing to take this show home ASAP. As amazing as my cock feels right now, I need to have it buried deep inside her pussy, claiming each and every inch of it as my own.

Sensing my urgency, Cassie quickens her pace. Stroking the underside of my shaft with her tongue as she gently squeezes my balls with her hand.

"Baby, if you keep doing that, you're going to make me blow in your mouth." A glance down and I see Cassie's wicked eyes dancing in mischief. "Ohhhhhh, my baby wants that."

I lick my lips in anticipation. *Shit, she's so fucking hot.* Just when I think this can't feel any more amazing, Cassie takes me deep into her throat, her lips touching the base of my cock as she swallows me down.

My whole body tingles as she hollows out her cheeks, the vibration of her moan making me see stars.

Over and over again, she pumps me with her gorgeous mouth, making my whole body tighten with the need to let go.

Cassie's big eyes look up at me and the emotion I see behind them is my undoing.

That's it. That's all she wrote. With a guttural roar, I release into her mouth, watching as the vixen who's stolen my heart swallows every last drop.

Thank fuck we're at a red light. I for sure would've wrecked.

Cassie sits up, and I've never seen a more beautiful sight. Her hair mussed, eyes glistening, and mouth swollen. Wiping at her mouth, I can't help but lean in and kiss her.

"You're everything, Cass," I whisper into her mouth as I pull away and put the car into drive once more.

After what feels like an eternity, we've finally reached the elevator to the penthouse. As soon as we're inside, I enter a code into the panel and the lights go out.

"What happened?"

"Shhhhh." The darkened elevator begins to ascend as I push her against the mirrored wall.

Lowering myself in front of her, I lift her ass onto the mid-rail, wrapping a leg around either side of my neck—effectively bringing me face-to-face with her wet pussy. I can practically feel the heat coming off of her.

Unable to resist, I push her drenched panties to the side and lick between her folds. "So fucking delicious."

Cassie knows what she wants and talking is not on the list. Grabbing on to my hair with both hands, she brings me back down onto her greedy cunt as she grinds into my mouth.

Before I can continue, the elevator pings, letting me know the doors are about to open, letting light spill in, and giving the closed-circuit cams a show I'm not willing to share.

Against Cassie's protest, I pull myself from her just in time for the doors to open. Not wanting to waste time, I pull her into my arms and carry her inside, bridal style.

Cassie narrows her eyes at me. "Have you ever done that before? How'd you know to shut the lights off in there?"

"No, little angel. You're the first. First in the elevator, first in my home, and most importantly, first in my heart."

ACTS OF SALVATION

My words silence her, and I swear I see a sheen of tears glistening in her eyes. Despite how tough she might act, I know this woman has a heart of gold. For fuck's sake, she's single-handedly supporting her mom while her asshole dad steps out on his woman.

"Ren, I..."

"Shhh. You don't have to say anything." I set her on the kitchen island, unable to wait any longer.

My mouth trails kisses from her lips, down her neck, and onto the swells of her breasts. Bringing both hands up to the dip in her cleavage, I take the fabric of her dress and rip right down the middle—exposing the most beautiful woman I've ever seen.

A gasp leaves her perfectly pouted lips, "That was an Alexander McQueen." Her hand trails down my abs, reaching my weeping dick and stroking me over my pants. "Good thing I already know you're worth it."

She shoots me a devilish grin as she squeezes my already impossibly hardened cock. A deep rumble emanates from my chest and she giggles, knowing full well what she's doing.

Finishing what I started, I take out my switchblade. Bringing it under the string of her thong, I pull up and toward me—making the material fall away, revealing heaven on earth.

"Beautiful." I'm about to lower myself back to her pink lips when Cassie stops me.

"No, I need you." Cassie takes charge, unbuttoning my pants, and taking me out.

"Fuck, I love that you know what you want." I bring her mouth to mine, issuing a punishing kiss.

Her tiny hand is still wrapped around my cock as she brings me to her opening, and as the tip of my cock touches her wetness, I lose all control.

With one forceful thrust, I'm inside, melting into her delicious walls.

With each push and pull, we become one. One movement, one breath, one heart, and one soul. Fuck if this doesn't feel perfect. I could live inside of her for the rest of my goddamn life and I wouldn't need for a thing.

Like red on a rose, this is where I belong.

Cassie's nails scraping down my back stir the beast inside, and it needs to claim her, mark her as mine. Wrapping her long flowing hair around my hand, I pull. Hard.

I grip her waist with my free hand, pumping in and out, watching myself disappear into nirvana. I swear this must be heaven because I've never felt anything sweeter.

Cassie brings her mouth to my forearm, biting down like a feral animal needing its release.

Knowing just what my baby likes, I bring my mouth down onto her nipple and suck hard. Scraping the hardened nub with my teeth, I release my other hand from her hair and trail it down her back, to the crevice between her ass.

Her body buckles beneath me as a lone finger traces the puckered circle of muscle before plunging into its depths, seeking my baby's reverie.

Right on cue, Cassie gushes onto my throbbing cock, and I revel as I watch her juices flow down onto me while she moans through her climax.

My turn.

I need her. Closer, harder, faster, marking her mine. Mine. Mine.

ACTS OF SALVATION

I pound into her mercilessly, needing more, needing everything. *She's* everything, She's *my* everything.

It's that thought that sends me spiraling into my own release.

Fuuuuuuuck. This is it. There's nothing left. Life beyond Cassie doesn't exist.

As I come down from the ultimate high, I know that my life will never be the same. Wherever I go, whatever I do, this woman needs to be a part of it—and I won't stop until that's not just a whispered prayer, but a truth.

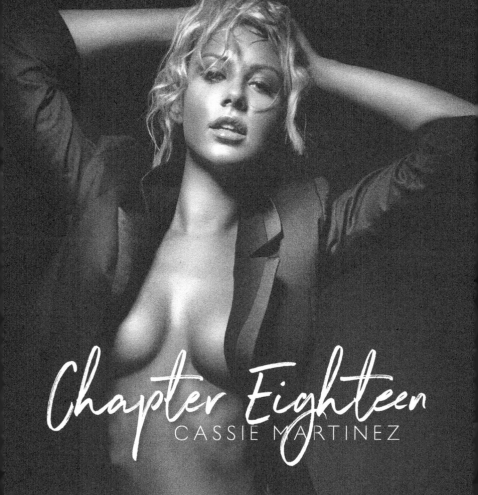

Chapter Eighteen
Cassie Martinez

DICK-WHIPPED. That's all I have to say.

My ass knew better than to lay with that man again. But did I listen? Nope. Like a calf to its slaughter, I went ready and willing.

I have nobody to blame but myself.

It's the morning after the end of the world as I know it, leaving me hungover as fuck though I didn't have a drop to drink.

Strolling into the kitchen, memories of what happened here last night come flashing back full force, making my whole body flush with arousal.

That was so damn hot. I've never reacted to a man the way I do with Ren, and that's terrifying. The amount of power he holds over me with just one touch is overwhelming.

Looking at the clock as I pour myself some coffee, I see that it's almost noon. Where's Ren? He left before the sun was fully up and still hasn't returned.

Checking my phone, I don't see any messages and the little devil on my shoulder begins to torment me. *What if he wasn't happy with what happened last night? What if it wasn't enough and he's now with Becca?*

Mentally snapping myself out of it, I tell myself I'm overreacting. Just as I'm about to dial Ren's number the door flings open and the look on his face is one of determination.

Ren heads straight for me, lifting me up and wrapping me around him like a blanket of limbs. "We've caught Bella's attacker." He breathes into my neck, running his nose along the sensitive skin and causing goose bumps to rise. "Well, more like attackers. Plural."

"Whaaat? Really?" I pull away just enough to see his face.

"Yes. Apparently, the attackers were in cahoots trying to clear millions from William's bank account, they just needed access to it." Ren trails a hand down my back, making me arch into him. "Since Bella was proving to be an obstacle, they tried scaring her."

There's more to the story, I can tell from his guarded expression, but I'm not wanting to ruin the moment by pushing him.

"Why don't you get ready. There's this food truck park I've been wanting to go to and I think you'll like it." Ren slides me off of him and the thought of food has my stomach grumbling.

"Sounds good, boss." I sashay back to the room with a wink.

"Boss, I like the sound of that." Ren's laughter trails off as I close the bathroom door, and I can't help but think that I could definitely get used to this.

Maybe domestic life isn't all that bad after all.

"What's that look for?" Ren asks as we enter the food truck park.

As the name dictates, it's a park with full-service food trucks lining the perimeter and a bunch of picnic tables and open space in the middle. There's a horseshoe toss to one side as well as some cornhole, and frisbee golf.

Not sure how smart it is to hand someone a frisbee where booze is being served.

"Thinking of Bella," I respond to Ren's question as my eye lands on a prosecco food truck. It looks like all they serve is bubbly. *Interesting.* "I sent her a message inviting her to come with us but she hasn't responded. Maybe I should stop by her place and check in on her." Looking at Ren I see something's up. "It's a big day, you know. I'd think she'd want to celebrate knowing her attacker is no longer a threat."

"Yea, I don't think that's going to be happening anytime soon. The cat's out of the bag about her and William, and let's just say my brother didn't take it too well."

"Oh my god! I should be with her right now! Why didn't you tell me sooner?!" My heart is racing a mile a minute. Here I am about to throw down some prosecco when my bestie is probably in tears.

"I didn't tell you because William has it handled." He grits his teeth, no doubt still trying to process that his little niece is with his best friend. "She's moving in with him and I thought it best to give them *space*." He spits out that last word as if it were pure vile.

"Don't make that face when you yourself have made me move in with you." I playfully shove at him. "That would be a little hypocritical, don't you think?"

Ren gives me a sheepish smile, letting me know I'm tearing down some of that disapproval. A girl has to help out wherever she can, even if it's only from the sidelines.

Feeling a little bit better about not being with Bella, I compromise with shooting her another text.

CASSIE: Hey girl, Ren told me about your old man... aaaand moving in with William! Just wanted to let you know that I'm here if you need anything. Love you, always and forever xoxo

She must have been on her phone because almost instantly I get a notification for an incoming text.

BELLA: Yesssss. Girl, so much has happened in the last twenty-four hours and we need a catch-up session, BAD. Especially, since it seems you need to fill me in on how my uncle has managed to give you the lowdown on something that happened not even ten hours ago.
Are you with him right now???

ACTS OF SALVATION

My eyes go wide and I can feel the color drain from my face.

Ren's voice cuts through my mental haze, "Baby, what's wrong? You look like you found out Prada went out of business." He smirks, rubbing his hands up and down my arms as if trying to revive me.

"Ha ha. Bella just asked me if I was with you right now and I froze." Just thinking of it again has my heart about to break out of my chest.

"Just tell her the truth. That you've moved in with me and you'll be staying there permanently." His tone is so matter-of-fact that he almost makes me believe things are as solid as he makes them out to be.

We weren't even on speaking terms a little over forty-eight hours ago and now it appears we are in a full-blown relationship, residing under the same roof, though be it temporary—much to Ren's dismay.

Talk about zero to sixty.

I'm about to answer with a rational breakdown of our courtship when a familiar face appears by Ren's side.

"Becca. What a surprise." I offer her a tepid smile, the best I can muster given our history.

Ren purses his lips to the side, trying to contain his laughter. Whatever. He can laugh all he wants, he just better not try and defend her catty ass.

"Hi, Becca. Did you come for the bahn mi truck?" Ren tries to direct the conversation to a much safer topic, like food—The man clearly doesn't know when a woman's claws have come out, they're out to play.

"Cassie, is it? I forgot to ask if you liked the flowers I ordered for you. I think they were pink peonies." As predicted, she ignores Ren's remark and attempts to go straight for the jugular. "I do all of Ren's floral requests."

The woman stands there with a self-satisfied smirk, thinking she's destroyed me with her implication. Well she's about to find out I'm not so easily messed with.

"Can't say that I remember what they were, to be honest. I was too busy reveling in having my man's fingers shoved deep in my pussy, making me come in ways that are positively sinful." I place a possessive hand on Ren's chest, trailing a finger over his heart. "It was almost as good as our stint in the elevator last night, wasn't it, baby?"

Ren, who is no longer trying to bite back his laughter, is outright chuckling. "Every time with you is the best time, baby." He removes his gaze from mine, and looking over to Becca, issues a disapproving glare. "If you'll excuse us, I'd like to take my girl over to my favorite truck."

"Well that wasn't tense at all." I look up at Ren as we walk toward the far side of the park. "That was sarcasm, in case you hadn't gathered."

"Oh, I gathered alright." Ren shakes his head as he brings a hand to the small of my back, causing a swarm of butterflies to take up residence in my stomach. "I don't know what's gotten into her. She's never been like that before."

"I think I've got an idea. Am I right in assuming you've never settled down with any of your past flings?"

"No... I haven't. I see what you're hinting at but I really don't think my relationship with Becca is like that. We've known each other for ages, and the one time we tried hooking up ended in a disaster."

"Wait." His words halt me in my tracks. "You've actually hooked up with that... that... that rude bitch?"

"Once, if you could call it that. I—"

I don't even let him finish the sentence, cutting him off with the mother of all tirades, "Spare me the details. Excuse me if I'm not keen on hearing about your endeavors with a woman who first of all, talked behind my back when she thought I didn't understand Spanish—and by the way, we still need to talk about how *you* actually know Spanish—and second of all, tried to downplay our relationship by insinuating she orders flowers for you on the regular, keeping your menagerie of women well stocked with florals."

Ren pulls me into his arms, squeezing me so hard I can barely breathe. "I love it when you're riled up like this. I'm tempted to take you home and skip the food."

"Did you hear a word I said?" I breathe into his chest, unable to break free from his hold and unsure if I really want to.

"Yes. And to answer your question, Spanish is extremely similar to Italian so I chose it as my elective in high school. I must say, it came in very handy over at your mom's yesterday." Ren finally pulls back enough for me to see his wicked smile.

I smack at his chest. "You brat. I had a feeling you knew what we were saying with how you were smiling. I guess it's no surprise my mom adores you."

Ren slides his hands down my back, cupping my ass and squeezing. "Not half as much as I adore you."

"Oh, yeah? And how much would that be?"

"Let's just say you should hold on to that old address book of hers. You might need it sooner than you think."

And with those words, Ren walks away, leaving me with my mouth wide open and shocked as hell.

Chapter Nineteen
REN MORETTI

POSTED UP ON THE U-shape sectional, we are two happy people, stuffed to the brim and in the presence of amazing company.

I smile, remembering Cassie throwing back the stuffed jalapeño poppers like they were skittles. I love the fact that she isn't a picky eater and doesn't count calories like most of the girls I've seen in the past.

Perfect. My little angel is fucking perfect.

On that note, I pick up one of the legs that are draped over my lap and begin to massage from her ankle down to her tiny foot.

"How do you walk on these? They're so small." I chuckle into the delicate skin of her ankle as I run a hand up her leg, reveling in the softness of her body. She's fit but still manages to keep curves in all the right places.

"Very funny. I'm short so I don't need massive boat feet like you." Her face flushes and I'm dying to know what she's thinking about. The vixen takes a finger to her mouth, biting down on it before admitting what was running through that dirty mind of hers, "It's true what they say... about big feet correlating to the size of a man's cock. At least with you."

Cassie withdraws her foot from my hand, gets up on all fours, and begins crawling toward me while biting her plump lower lip. Instantly, my dick hardens, pressing against the seam of my jeans and wanting out.

God, how I love living with this woman.

Cassie straddles me, lowering her face to mine, brushing our noses together, leaving our lips just within hovering distance. I can't help but seek her mouth out with my tongue. I need to touch her, taste her, consume her.

I run my tongue across her juicy lower lip and my cock jumps against her apex as it remembers what those lips were doing last night. Visions of Cassie sucking me off, drinking every last drop I had, and enjoying every bit of it.

My chest swells with an emotion I've never felt before, making me stop what I'm doing.

"You okay there, big guy?" Cassie's look of concern puts me on notice.

I *will not* kill the mood with my stupid heart.

"What could possibly be wrong? I have the most beautiful

woman grinding on me like I'm her own personal sex toy."

"But you are, aren't you? Mine and only mine?" The vulnerability in her eyes slays me, urging me to give her the security she so clearly needs.

"Of course, my little angel. Yours and yours alone." I want to add always and forever, but this girl is so skittish she's bound to hop off and put an end to our fun.

Her smile regains some of that confidence I love so much. It's like lighter fluid, further igniting whatever fire I've had, and shooting up ten-foot flames of desire, enveloping us in their heat.

Needing more, I lift her off and lay her down on her back, removing the summer dress she's been teasing me with all day.

Immediately, my eyes gravitate toward her tits. Absolute perfection. The perfect handful with dusky pink nipples begging to be sucked. Happy to oblige, I palm a breast, bringing my mouth down and rolling the nipple with my tongue before gently biting down.

Cassie releases a moan as she wraps her legs around me, rolling her heat against my aching cock.

"I need you." She breathes into the space between us. The scent of her a drug, making my synapsis fire and forever ingraining it as the smell of home.

"My baby gets what my baby wants." I quickly pull myself free, eager to be back inside her, where I belong.

Slowly, I lower myself to her entrance, rubbing the pearl of precum from my slit onto her clit—*back and forth*.

The sight before me is enough to make me blow, making me use every bit of restraint I possess to hold back—Cassie playing with her tits as her head tilts back in ecstasy is a sight to behold.

Taking a mental picture, I forever ingrain this moment into my mind before slamming into her without warning, taking her, making her mine once more.

Heaven. No other word could do this feeling justice.

Never in my life have I felt anything sweeter. Savoring the moment, I take my time watching myself slide in and out, her slick juices leaving me glistening with the evidence of her desire.

So beautiful, the union of our bodies speaking a silent language only we can understand. She must be enjoying it as much as I am because without preamble, her walls start clamping down on my shaft, letting me know my little angel is about to explode.

My brows shoot up as I bite my lip in a poor attempt at keeping myself from full-blown grinning at this revelation.

Cassie glares at my antics as she pulls me down, rolls me over, and begins to roll her hips into me, grinding her clit onto the skin where our bodies meet.

Wanting to make her lose her mind, I angle my hips up, hitting that spot deep inside her and assaulting her senses completely, letting her be as consumed with me as I am with her.

I know my baby well, and like clockwork, she begins to squeeze me, milking me for all I'm worth. Unable to hold back any longer, we release at the same time, making magic.

Fucking magic.

As I feel myself spill into her I'm reminded that for the second time, we've had sex without a condom. Strangely, I'm not freaking out. On the contrary, visions of Cassie carrying our baby, makes my dick twitch in excitement.

This is unheard of for me. From a young age, our father taught us the importance of wrapping it up. With the Moretti name comes great responsibility. I know there are a number of shameless women who'd try to bag my brother or me for our money, and they most certainly wouldn't bat a lash at using less than honorable means.

"Baby, I'm sorry. I forgot to put something on." I know that having this conversation while I'm still inside her isn't ideal, but I want to let her know that I'm here for her no matter what. "Just know that whatever happens, I'm okay with it."

Cassie smacks my shoulder. "Real smooth, Casanova. I'm on the pill so we're good on that front, and I'm clean. Are you?" She cocks a brow, no doubt referencing my prior wayward ways.

"Yes. I just had a physical and I've never been bare with anyone before. I would never knowingly put you in danger. You're too precious to me."

Something flashes in her eyes, too quickly for me to discern. I slide out of her, cleaning her up with my shirt.

"You okay?"

"Yes, I'm good." Her words are meant to comfort me but they do little to put me at ease when her demeanor is so at odds with what she's saying.

I bring her onto my lap, stroking her back like one would a startled creature. "Talk to me baby, what's going through that head of yours."

"It's nothing, really." She presses her lips together while bringing her knees to her chest, letting me know she's closing herself off once more. "I should probably go to bed. I have to pull a bunch of pieces for the Wilson family. They have an event coming up soon and I want to run the selections by Blair tomorrow morning."

Her words hit me like a slap to the face. "You're not still

wanting to work with McCreepster are you? That guy's a fucking douche." Memories of his hands on her has me wanting to break things.

"I sort of have to. I have a contract, remember?" She cocks her head to the side, looking up at me as if I were dense.

"Of course I remember, but I told you I'd have our attorney look at it. He's already combing through it and will no doubt have a loophole for you within the next couple of days."

"Okay, well until then, I have a job to fulfill." She pops off my lap, picking up her dress from the floor and turning around to issue another metaphorical slap. "Any word from the cleaning crew? Is my place ready for me to move back in?"

I sit there stunned. Unable to form words for a minute. The ache in my chest feels raw, as if she's just ripped it open with her bare fucking hands.

We'd just shared what was arguably one of, if not *the most* intimate moments of my life and here she is, desperately clawing to get away from me.

To leave me.

"No. I haven't heard, but I promise I'll let you know as soon as they call me." I don't smile. There's nothing happy about this moment and there's no sense in bullshitting.

I've never been one to fake shit and I'm not about to start now. I've also never been one to grovel, and if Cassie doesn't want what I've so clearly offered, then I'm not going to force it.

Maybe my brother *was* right.

I've let one other woman in and when she left me, it wrecked my world. I'm not about to let it happen again.

Chapter Twenty
CASSIE MARTINEZ

I MESSED UP. I know I did.

It's the morning after my non-fight fight with Ren and all I can do is keep replaying that look of hurt across his face.

There I was, in the arms of an amazing man, and what did I do? I fucking spat in his face. Metaphorically of course, but still.

I knew he'd been wanting me to move in, but that whole bit about him not wanting me to work with the Wilson family freaked me out. It reminded me of when my dad told my mom she couldn't go to night school because he was afraid the teacher was hitting on her.

It all sort of spiraled from there. Next thing I knew instead of going for round two of mind-blowing sex I was telling him I'd be leaving. Once the words were out, I knew there'd be no taking them back.

I knew how much my not moving in would hurt him, but I just couldn't help myself. My self-defense mechanism kicked in and now that I've made my bed I need to lay in it.

Letting out a deep sigh, I go over the last-minute selections I've pulled for the Wilson family. I'm sitting in the circular driveway of their estate—about to close my laptop—when there's a tap on my window.

Looking up I see Dr. Wilson's murky brown eyes, staring at me like a man starving for his next meal. Chills run up my spine and all I can do is try and remind myself of my mom and all of her expenses.

I hold up one finger, making a show of getting my bag together when in reality I just need a minute to compose myself after his stare-down.

Finally stepping out of the car, I let myself officially greet him. "Good morning, Dr. Wilson."

"Cassie, please, just call me Woodrow. I'd think we're past formalities by now."

"Right, Woodrow. I take it your wife and children are inside?" I make my way around him and begin walking toward the home.

"Blair stepped out real quick, something about her emergency stash of La Crue being out. You know her and her chardonnay." He offers me a half-hearted chuckle when we both know there's nothing funny about his wife's drinking habit. "And the kids are in their play area with the nanny."

Wonderful. I have the charmer all to myself. I mentally roll my eyes, sending up a prayer that by some miracle he manages to behave.

My hopes are short-lived. As soon as the front door closes behind us, I feel his sweaty palm run down the exposed skin of my back. I'm wearing another halter dress and there's plenty of skin for him to choose from since I have my back to him.

Not wanting to give him another opening, I whirl around in place.

I hadn't thought my actions through because in turning around so quickly, his hand automatically slid from the exposed skin on my back to the side of my breast, and you know the McCreeperson doesn't allow for a missed opportunity.

He quickly squeezes, before I'm able to step back, pulling away from his grasp and finally out of his reach.

Shuddering in revulsion, I'm standing there, mouth agape. "Dr. Mc... I mean Dr. Wilson. That is *not* acceptable."

"What isn't acceptable?" Blair walks in from the hallway, glass of chardonnay in hand and it's not even nine a.m.

This whole scene has me rethinking my argument with Ren last night. Maybe he was right, and I was just overreacting because not working for the Wilson's is sounding like the best idea ever right now.

Dr. Wilson cuts into my thoughts, "Oh, that Barbie wanted to pull her contact information from the directory instead of asking for it directly. You can never be too sure these days so I thought it best if I asked Cassie one-on-one if she was okay with Barbie calling her on her personal line."

The lie flows so easily, I wonder if he's had a lot of experience keeping things from his wife. Not knowing what to say I just stand there and openly stare, focusing on the glass of golden liquid in Blair's hand.

"Ahhhh, yes. I never pegged Barbie for a lesbian. But whatever floats her boat."

My mouth hangs open for the second time this morning. How could this woman be so clueless? Barbie is as much a lesbian as Blair is sober.

Not that there's anything wrong with being gay. Love is love.

No, it's this woman's blatant ignorance that leaves me completely flabbergasted.

"Well, Cassie? Is it okay for me to give Barbie your information? She was hoping to set up a bit of a coffee date with you." Dr. Wilson looks at me expectantly.

Blinking away my fog, I quickly answer. "Yes, that's fine. It shouldn't be a problem. Barbie is really nice."

"A little *too* nice," Blair mumbles into her glass.

I clear my throat before stepping into the lounge, "I've brought the selections for the debutante ball where your niece will be presented. Shall we go over your choices first?"

In all reality, I *need* to get her selection while she's still coherent. Not to mention I also want to be as far away from Dr. McCreeperson as possible right now.

"Very well." Blair sloshes her drink in the direction of the chaise. "Let's sit. I'll pick."

Gladly taking the reprieve from Mr. Handsy, I sit, opening my laptop and pulling up her options.

ACTS OF SALVATION

I'm turning onto Oak Lawn and as far away from the Wilson family as possible.

Talk about dysfunctional.

I pull over into this cute little coffee shop needing a caffeine fix ASAP. My lack of sleep and this morning's drama combined have me jonesing for a pick-me-up.

I'm about to order a double espresso when my phone lights up and I see that it's Bella.

"Hey girl, what's up?"

"Did I just see you pull into Vinnie's off Oak Lawn?" Bella's voice is high-pitched, letting me know she's excited.

"Yeeeesss, are you stalking me now?" I tease, knowing her new home is a mere mile down the road.

"You know it. Now order me a cappuccino. I'm turning around. Be there in a sec." The line goes dead before I have a chance to protest.

Don't get me wrong, it's not that I don't want to spend time with my best friend, I'm just not keen on spilling the beans as it pertains to her uncle and me—and let's face it, Bella will stop at nothing to pry information from me if she smells blood in the water.

Not even five minutes later, the bell above the door rings, notifying the room of Bella's arrival. Waving her over to the table I snagged, I decide to keep as much under wraps as possible.

Not because I don't trust her, but because I don't even have the whole situation sorted in my head. Hell, I don't even know whether

Ren and I are even a thing—especially after last night.

"*God*, are you a sight for sore eyes." Bella pulls the cappuccino toward her, embracing the mug with a two-handed hold and bringing it up to her lips.

"I'd say nice to see you too, but I think that greeting was for the coffee and not for me." I grin while shaking my head side to side. "You and your love affair with caffeine."

"You know it. Coffee is my first love, then comes William." Bella winks as she lifts the mug to her lips for another sip.

"Speaking of... How are you settling into your new home? I mean, I know you were living there before when you were caring for Harper full time, but now you're in the master instead of the guest room." I waggle my brows playfully.

"It's bittersweet. I love being with William, officially, out in the open without having to sneak around—but having my dad disown me and cut me off from the twins... well, it sucks donkey balls, to put it mildly."

"He'll come around... Eventually. I hate to say this, but he's been a very selfish father. It's time you worried about your own happiness for once instead of running around and playing mom to your little brothers." I can tell my words are making Bella uncomfortable. She's always had this misplaced sense of guilt after her mother's death, tarnishing every action or decision she's made since then. "Look, all I'm saying is that your dad will come around. So for now, take this time to take care of yourself. Heal, be happy, and grow."

"You're right, it's just easier said than done." Bella picks at her nails. "Aaaanyway. Why don't you tell me how you got the lowdown on my living situation so quickly? And from my uncle, no less."

My face heats up and I know I can't tell Bella everything, so I go with a version of the truth. "I didn't want to tell you anything because you've had a lot going on yourself. But a couple of nights ago, someone broke into my place and completely trashed it—with dog poo."

Bella's brows lift and her eyes go as wide as saucers. "I'm sorry, did you just say *dog poo*?"

"Yup. And they also left pictures of me with the eyes scratched out." Bella's mouth is hanging open by this point, and I don't blame her one bit. "That whole incident was totally creepy, to say the least."

Bella nods emphatically. "Okay, so go on. What does this have to do with my uncle and who do they think committed such a twisted crime?"

Should've known she wasn't going to drop it.

"He reached out to me, letting me know he wasn't sure to what extent your attacker would go, so he thought it smart to have someone posted up at my place every night. Reluctantly, I agreed. It's no big secret I don't live in the safest of neighborhoods, right?"

"No, but it's the price you must pay to live in such a cool loft like yours. I absolutely love the exposed brick and industrial feel." Her pleasant smile turns downward as she reaches over and grabs my hand. "I am so sorry you had to go through that mess because of me and the drama that is my life. Seriously, don't ever feel like I have too much going on for you. You're like my sister and there isn't anything I wouldn't drop to come be by your side—even William." The smile is back full force, and it warms my aching heart.

"I love you too, Bella." Though she didn't quite say those words, I know it's what she meant. It also digs the blade of guilt that much deeper, knowing she's given such a big piece of her heart to me and I can't even come clean about Ren.

I remind myself that I have my reasons. And the main reason is probably at home right now, waiting on me to apologize for last night.

"Okay, I love you too but you still haven't told me what all that has to do with Ren." Bella purses her lips, waiting for an explanation that actually makes sense.

"He was worried about my safety so he had me stay with him for a couple of days. But now that the attacker is caught, I can go back home."

Bella's jaw is practically on the table. "Oh my god, Cassie. You know he's never let another woman stay at his place. Like *ever*."

"Right, but I'm not the usual guest. It's not like he was wining and dining me." With those words, the blade of guilt digs in a little deeper. *Food trucks don't count as wining and dining, do they?*

Bella purses her lips to the side, probably questioning whether there's any validity to my statement. "I guess that could be possible." She narrows her eyes while bringing her mug to her lips, hovering it a mere millimeter away before asking the million-dollar question. "How do *you* feel about my uncle?"

My heart begins to pound so hard in my chest, I can hear it in my ears. The beat is so loud I wonder if Bella can hear it too.

"I love Ren." The words flow casually and freely, as if I've said them a million times before.

Bella spits out the mouthful of coffee she'd just sipped. "You *what?*"

Immediately realizing what I've said, I try to slap a Band-Aid on the situation. "Relax. I meant I love Ren like I love puppies or a long hot bath." I try to school my features in an attempt to hide my internal freakout. I *cannot* believe I just said that.

"Right. Right." Bella dabs at her mouth with a napkin. "Sorry, you just caught me off-guard there. I mean, I wouldn't be opposed to the idea of you and my uncle."

Now it's Bella's turn to waggle her brows, meanwhile, mine are scrunching together. "You wouldn't? I mean, he's like a decade and a half older... *and your uncle.*" As soon as the words are out, I realize how ridiculous they are given the fact that Bella is currently shacking up with an older man herself. Well, at least the uncle thing still stands.

Bella's brows raise, "Seriously?! You do know William went to high school with Ren, Right?" She smiles while shaking her head. "Anyway. I don't mind at all, chickadee. I mean, how cool would it be if we were officially family. You'd be my auntie!" Bella cackles, attracting multiple sets of eyes to our table.

I can't help but smile at the extent of her acceptance, but that still doesn't mean I can lay out the details of what's really happened. At least not yet. I need to make sure there's actually something there before getting her hopes up.

"Speaking of your uncle. I need to head over to his place to pick up my stuff now that your psycho attacker has been caught." I chuckle as I get up to hug her goodbye. "Poor Bruce is going to have a hard time leaving the lap of luxury and settling back down into our humble abode."

Bella hugs me before pulling away and arching a brow. "You *could* just stay with Uncle Ren?"

ELEANOR ALDRICK

Yet another person suggesting I move in with a man I barely know. I shake my head as I silently laugh. *Et tu, Brute?*

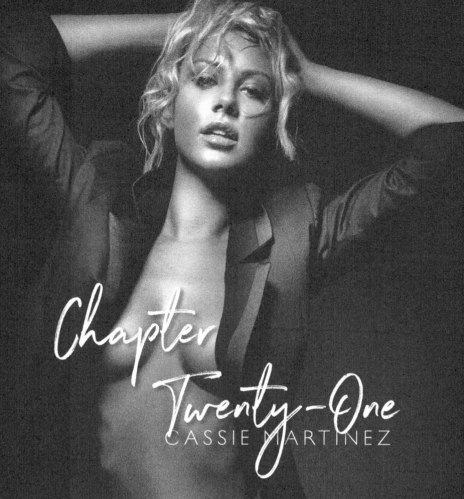

Chapter Twenty-One
CASSIE MARTINEZ

I'M DRAGGING MY feet as I make my way to the penthouse elevator. Let's just say apologizing isn't my forte. Just as the doors shut, my phone begins to vibrate.

Looking down, I see I have a message from my sister Aria reminding me of our family dinner tonight. It vibrates in quick succession once more, and a message pops up letting me know Ren's presence is being requested.

I let out a groan as I lean against the cool mirrored wall of the elevator. *Ugh.* Will he even want to come after what I did to him last night? The poor guy basically laid his heart out, and what did I do?

Step on it—with five-inch stiletto heels.

The elevator doors open onto the penthouse floor and what stands before me sends my stomach through Olympic level somersaults. Becca, with a smug as fuck smile on her face.

She's dressed in a pencil skirt that's practically painted on, and a white button-up blouse that's showing way too much cleavage to be demure. I don't miss the fact that the first couple of buttons aren't aligned correctly, as if she had to dress quickly.

My stomach turns into a fifty-pound bowling ball, and I'm pretty sure there's no hiding the displeasure in my face.

"Cassie. Good afternoon." She nods once while stepping into the elevator I'm still standing in.

Getting my ass in gear, I step into the penthouse foyer and don't return her half-ass greeting. As soon as I hear the elevator doors close, I'm off in search of the man who she was definitely here to see.

A minute later, I find Ren situated in the leather wingback chair behind his massive mahogany desk. For such a modern apartment, William's office is like stepping back in time. The walls are lined with custom-designed bookshelves, the detailed millwork is exquisite, and the old-fashioned ladder that glides from one end of the wall to the other leaves no room for question that this is indeed a book lovers' home.

"Cassie." Ren's facial expression is detached, no emotion to be seen. "Did you come to pick up your things? Bruce is in the master bedroom, last I saw." He returns his gaze to the folder in his hand, dismissing me from the conversation.

Well, shit. He's really mad. Is that why he had Becca up here? Focus, Cassie. Just apologize and move on. "I'm sorry."

ACTS OF SALVATION

Those two words have Ren looking back up at me, his eyes narrowing and brows scrunching together. "What exactly are you sorry for?"

I should've known better than to think this was going to be easy.

"For how I acted last night."

"And how did you act last night?"

Jesus. He isn't making this any easier, is he?

"Like someone who was scared shitless." I shift on my feet awkwardly. Not knowing where to place my arms, I cross them over my chest. "Look, Ren, I'm not a normal girl who gets all starry-eyed and giggly when the guy she's seeing mentions moving in together. I'm also not the type of girl who likes to be controlled. I'm an independent woman and any man who wants to be with me needs to realize that he can't dictate who I can and cannot work for or where I can and cannot live."

Ren's face morphs from serious to amused. His lips are pursed to the side and I can tell he's fighting a smile. There's no hiding the playful light in his eyes.

"What else is this man of yours going to need to do?" That beautiful mouth of his splits into a wide grin that's contagious.

"Give me some time. Time to get used to the idea of a relationship."

Ren gets up from his chair and rounds his desk, heading straight for me. Reaching out both hands, he cups my face, tilting it up to his. "Does my little angel need anything else from her man?"

My whole body flushes at the multiple thoughts that race through my mind, all of them naughty. But what comes out of my mouth is completely unexpected for the both of us, "Keep Becca out of the apartment."

Ren's whole body tenses and I can see the wheels in his head turning. "You know that Becca is just my secretary, right? Did you bump into her on your way up, is that what this is about?" Ren's hands drop from my face down to the small of my back as he pulls me into him. "She delivers files whenever I'm working from home. Seriously, there's nothing for you to worry about there."

Images of Becca's inappropriately buttoned blouse come to mind, and I know that it's not exactly proof of anything, but I can't help but ask myself '*what if?*'

Noticing that I haven't said a word and that my eyes have suddenly landed on every surface in the room except for him, Ren pulls me in tighter, depositing a kiss to the top of my head. "Hey, baby. It's only you, okay? Always you."

"Mhm," I mumble into his chest. "While we're at it, there's one more request I'd like to tack on for the night."

"Oh this is just the list for the night?" Ren laughs, his chest rising and falling beneath my hands. "Okay, let's have it. What's the request?"

"Dinner with my family." I give him a sheepish smile and bat my lashes in an exaggerated manner. "You know you want to." I poke at his side before we both burst into laughter.

"I'd actually really like that." Ren musses my hair, before slapping my ass and walking away. "But first, how about you join me in the shower?"

ACTS OF SALVATION

A couple of hours later, after we're both thoroughly cleaned, we find ourselves in the comfort of his blacked-out SUV.

"Do all of the men of WRATH own one of these? I could've sworn I saw William driving the exact same car."

"Yes, and they all come decked out with bulletproof glass too. Never know when the crazies will come out." Ren winks while reaching a hand out and squeezing my thigh.

"Are you calling me crazy?" I laugh, knowing full well that after last night he probably thinks I definitely have a couple of screws loose.

"I'm not the one who said it." He shrugs his shoulders while grinning like a fool.

Smacking his shoulder, I can't help but join in and grin myself. I could definitely get used to this.

Ren pulls into a gas station on the south side of Dallas. "Need to fill'er up. Want anything from inside?"

"Nope, I'm good thanks." I watch him as he exits the car and makes his way into the convenience store—that's when I notice it. *The tree.*

Holy shit. I haven't been back here in ages. My mom used to wait tables at the taqueria attached to the gas station and I'd have to sit inside and wait for hours. Some days, when the store was really busy, my mom would give me a dollar for ice cream and let me sit outside under that tree.

I quickly get out of the car, needing to see if it still has all the wishes I'd carved into it. It was my very own wish tree, and whatever I carved into it *had* to come true.

My god... they're all here. I run my fingers over the worn-out markings, marveling at the imagination I once possessed.

ELEANOR ALDRICK

There's the one where I asked for my parents to stop fighting. I roll my eyes. Not even God himself could make that happen, let alone a tree.

Oh my god, there's the one where I asked for bigger boobs. My mouth curves into a wide grin. Okay, that one was really funny.

My eyes are suddenly drawn a few inches down. It's just as old as the others, but it's the name signed below it that sticks out... *Ren.*

I crouch down, needing to read the engraving.

As I begin to read, my body tingles with awareness. Not a moment later, I feel him. His hand covering mine as we trace the writing on the tree.

Turning around, I see Ren's eyes, flickering back and forth between mine, glittering with unshed tears.

"Cassie, *my little angel.*" His eyes are now full of wonder and something else I can't describe. Gratitude?

As if in a time warp, those same eyes appear before me.
Only they belong to a very drunk and very young Ren, laying under this very tree.
Mom had just given me my spending money, and I'd chosen a delicious ice cream cone as my treat.
Cone in hand, I was happier than a pig in mud and on my way to the wishing tree. That's when I spotted the handsome stranger in my spot. I must've been eight at the time, but even I knew what a drunk man looked like, and he was definitely drunk.
Something in his eyes told me he needed a friend, and even though I'd been taught to stay away from strangers, I thought he was worth investigating.
"Hello, mister. Are you okay?"

ACTS OF SALVATION

"Is anyone ever really okay?" The man takes a pull from a bottle nestled inside a paper bag before running a filthy hand over his face.

Even drunk and filthy I could see that he was extremely handsome. I wonder how he got like this, and if he's going to be okay.

I plop down next to him, needing to help him if I can.

"Mom says as long as you still have breath, then you're still okay." I stick a finger under the stranger's nose. "Yup. Looks like you still have breath, mister."

The man laughs a full-bellied laugh. "Do you typically go sticking your fingers under people's noses, little girl?"

"No. But you seemed like you needed it." I take a lick of my ice cream before pointing to my tree. "This is my tree and it's special. I think that's why God brought you here—to make a wish on my special wishing tree."

A lone tear falls down the man's tired face and I reach up to wipe it away. "Why are you so sad, mister? Maybe the tree can make it all better."

He chuckles, throwing his head back and closing his eyes. "If only it could." The man brings his face back to mine before hitting me with the saddest words an eight-year-old could possibly hear. "My mother died. She was sick for a very long time." He presses his lips together, closing his eyes once more. "And she finally chose to leave us last night."

Overcome with emotion, I fling myself at the man, tossing my ice cream to the side and hugging him as tight as my little arms can squeeze. "She's with God now. She isn't sick anymore. Nobody in heaven is sick. They're all happy and get to eat ice cream all day long."

I feel the man choke back a sob, so I know I still have more work to do. "Mom said that when our loved ones pass away, like my abuelito, they go on to heaven and become our guardian angels. That way, they never really leave us. And if we're real quiet and hold real still, we can even feel their love."

The man pulls me away enough so that I can see his face. "Where did you come from, little angel?"

Looking deep into his eyes, I know this to be true. "I think your guardian angel sent me."

The man's face contorts as if he were in physical pain and his eyes are now leaking a multitude of silent tears. Wiping at his face, the man sniffles. "How about we make that wish now?"

He takes out a pocket knife, much sharper than the pen I always carry with me to sketch.

"What's your wish gonna be, mister?"

"You tell me, little angel." He smiles, showing off a dimple that makes me feel warm all over.

I think real hard because it needs to be a good one. Closing my eyes, I listen like my momma taught me, and let myself feel the love. That's it! That's what he needs! My eyes flash open, wanting to share the wish as soon as possible.

"**May I always feel the love of my angel, carrying it forever in my heart.**"

I nod once, knowing that's exactly what he needs to wish

for. "That way, you'll never feel alone or lost, and you'll never be this sad again."

The man takes in a deep breath, letting it out slowly as he nods. "That's perfect, little angel. Fucking perfect."

He quickly takes his pocket knife to the tree, scribing the wish onto its bark and sealing it with his name.

- Ren.

A cool breeze hits me, bringing attention to the wetness on my cheeks. *I've been crying.* And a quick glance up lets me know that Ren remembers too.

His face says it all but it's the words that come next that confirm it, "My *little angel.*"

I nod, my mouth slightly ajar.

"You were sent to me, specifically for me, and I can't see myself spending another day without you." Grabbing my face in both of his hands, he brings us closer. "What do you say, little angel, will you marry me?"

His question hits me like a freight train. Never in a million years did I think I'd be proposed to, let alone at a gas station with a man I apparently met over a decade ago.

Flashes of my mom and dad fly before me. All of their fights, all of the times I've had to bail Mom out when Dad's taken all her money. As soon as those images slow, I'm hit again with visions of Aria, crying about her asshole of a fiancé and how she's sure he's sleeping around.

That's when the memory of Becca and her disheveled blouse pops up unbidden.

I can't breathe. The world starts spinning and I'm pretty sure the wishing tree is swaying heavily. *Shit, I think that's me.* I think

I'm the one who's swaying.

If it weren't for Ren holding me up, I'm pretty sure I'd be laid out on the ground.

"I can't," I blurt out. "I need air."

I don't have time to process Ren's facial expression. All I know is I need to get away. I need everything to just slow down and stop spinning.

Ren practically carries me back to the SUV and I'm not sure if he's even said anything up until this point. All I know is that my heart is still pounding in my head and my eyes haven't stopped leaking.

As soon as he's back behind the wheel, I blurt out, "Please drop me off at Mom's."

Through my periphery, I see him nod before starting the ignition. From the silence in the car, I think it's safe to say he knows I wasn't inviting him along.

It's really not my intention to hurt him, but I honestly can't even deal with my own thoughts right now. Attempting to smooth things over, I open my mouth to speak, "Ren, I—"

"Don't," he cuts me off before I can even finish my sentence. "I know proposing at a gas station is probably not the best move, and fuck, Cass, we're not even officially dating..." Ren runs his hand through his hair, tugging at the ends. "Look, I'll just take you to your mom's."

I lay my head against the coolness of the window and close my eyes. The past twenty-four hours have been overwhelmingly emotional, and the saddest part is, I'm not sure my heart is strong enough to survive.

Chapter Twenty-Two
CASSIE MARTINEZ

THE RIDE TO MOM'S was a silent one. Can't say that I blame him. I'd just shot him down in the worst way. I knew he was guarded, never giving himself freely to anyone, and yet I still couldn't bring myself to tell him what he wanted to hear.

Not because I didn't want to. *Fuck, I'd give anything to be his happily ever after.* But because I'm just not sure that scenario even really exists.

Agreeing to marriage would be agreeing to failure, wouldn't it?

"*Levantate.*" Mom hits me over the head with a pillow, telling me to get up.

It's the morning after the proposal and I'm laid out on her vinyl-covered couch. As if the velvet floral pattern underneath wasn't outdated enough, she had to go and stick plastic over the whole thing.

"Okay, okay, Ma. I'm up." I sit up, peeling myself from the couch, sticky from having perspired over the night.

"So, are you going to tell me why you stayed here, in my home instead of the spacious apartment with the handsome man you were supposed to bring over for dinner last night?" She takes a seat next to me, holding my gaze with a look that leaves no room for lies.

Taking in a deep breath, I let it out before I lose the nerve. "He proposed."

Mom shoots up like a rocket and immediately begins to pace back and forth. "*Dios mio!* What a blessing! I never thought you'd marry. Now you can give me grandbabies!"

I swear I think there are tears in her eyes. *Well, this is going to be awkward.*

"Mom, first of all, you don't need any more grandbabies. Carmen has you set for life. Second of all, I didn't exactly say yes."

Mom stops her pacing and stares at me, slack-jawed. "*Pero,* why? That man looked at you like he was worshiping the moon. Not to mention he's very handsome and would give you beautiful babies."

"Again with the babies, Ma. Don't you get enough cuddles when the kids come over? I know Carmen has you watching them at least twice a week."

"Stop changing the subject and tell me why you let such a good man walk away." She sits back down, pulling my hands into hers.

I take another deep breath and release another truth. "I'm

scared. I've never wanted to get married. All I've ever seen is failure when it comes to marriage and relationships. I guess I just didn't want to be another statistic. Another shattered soul among the many broken hearts."

"Oh, Cassandra. I'm sorry I couldn't be a better example for you." She shakes her head as she runs a hand over my unkempt hair. "But not all stories are as tragic as mine. Look at Carmen, she's happily married to the love of her life, and has five beautiful children to show for it."

I scoff. "Oh please, Carmen follows that man around like a lovesick puppy, catering to his every want and need."

Mom tsks, "That's love, Cassie. Do you see that Hernando also does the same for her? He spoils that woman rotten, any way he can. When you love someone completely, that's what you do, you want to give them the world."

Something stirs in my chest, and I know that it's because her words resonate with my own truth. From the time I was eight, all I wanted to do was bring Ren peace and happiness. But instead, all I've done is hurt him time and time again because of my damn fear.

It's my turn to shake my head at myself. If only I could kick my own ass, too. "God, Ma. Why was I so stupid?" Burying my face in my hands, I vow to try to make things right between Ren and me.

"We aren't perfect, *mija*. Even Carmen and her husband have their problems. The trick is choosing who's worth the fight. That one decision has the power to give you the love of a lifetime—if you're brave enough to try."

A tear escapes me, and I realize I'm crying yet again. *Jesus.* I've managed to reign in my emotions for over a decade, but give me twenty-four hours with Ren and I'm a blubbering mess.

Mom kisses me on the forehead before wiping at my cheek. "Why don't you go clean up, have some breakfast, and then go get that man of yours. Okay?"

"Okay." I smile, taking in a clearing breath and getting myself in gear to deliver the mother of all apologies. Lord knows it's going to be one hell of a doozie.

I'm nervously chewing on my lip as the penthouse elevator ascends to its final destination where a big fat piece of humble pie awaits.

I can only hope that he accepts my apology. No man wants to have their marriage proposal rejected, and especially not have it induce a panic attack and tears of horror.

Mentally steeling myself for what's to come, I smooth down the front of my dress and stand tall.

No matter what happens, I'll be okay.

Repeating my mantra, I step out of the elevator and into the foyer where I have a clear view of the kitchen... *and Becca... without her top.*

My breakfast threatens to come back up as I stand there, clenching my jaw, unsure of what to do or say next.

Becca, however, is the epitome of calm and collected. She brings a coffee mug up to her lips and takes a sip before casually lifting her eyes to mine.

"Cassie, come to join us for our morning coffee?"

The shower that'd been running in the background shuts off and I know it's only a matter of minutes before Ren comes strutting in with his post-orgasmic glow.

I almost vomit right then and there, but Bruce comes bursting into the foyer, jumping up onto his hind legs, greeting me with the enthusiasm of a toddler on a sugar high.

"Down boy." I manage a small laugh, thankful for this beast that's always been able to make the darkest of moments better. "We were together last night. You'd think we hadn't seen each other in ages."

I scratch behind his ear before grabbing his leash and doggy bag out of the coat closet. Doggy supplies in hand and elevator call button pushed, I turn to face the smug bitch who's undoubtedly been watching my every move.

"Please tell Ren that I'll send someone for the rest of my things." The elevator doors slide open and I'm thankful for at least one thing going my way this morning.

At the very least, the quick exit will help me save a little face and let me break down in the comfort of my own car.

As soon as the door to my jeep closes, the dam of tears I'd been holding back breaks free.

The first emotion to hit is rage. *Did what we share mean so little to him?*

God, I'm such a damn hypocrite. That's probably what he was thinking last night when I tore his heart in two.

I fucked up. Bad. And this is what I get... but did he have to move on so quickly?

My head can't make sense of anything right now. Banging my

head on the steering wheel, one word keeps spinning on a loop over and over again, like a broken record.

Stupid, stupid, stupid. So fucking stupid.

My first mistake was thinking that I could have any semblance of a normal relationship. My second mistake was allowing Ren to creep into my heart. My third mistake was the horrible way I handled things last night.

I'll be damned if I'm stuck making any more foolish mistakes. This morning's run-in was an eye-opener.

No more putting my stupid heart on the line. I wasn't built for shit like this.

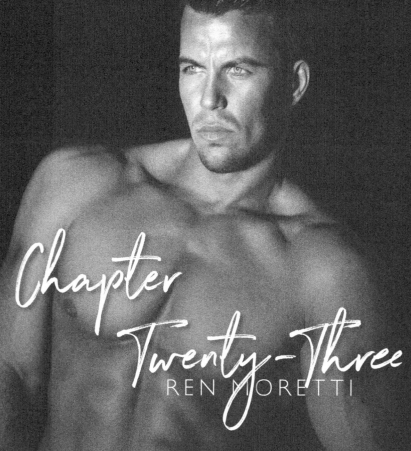

Chapter Twenty-Three
REN MORETTI

I T'S BEEN A WEEK since Cassie stopped by my place to pick up Bruce. I can't believe she just took him without saying goodbye.

My chest tightens at the memory of Cass beneath the tree. *Our tree. My little angel.*

"Ren, did you hear what I said?" Titus' tone of annoyance brings me back to my surroundings. I'm back at the Dallas office after a week in California, covering for the client Aiden was supposed to be in charge of.

"No, man. What did you say?"

"The prints, from Cassie's apartment." He lets out an exasperated breath.

Well, he certainly has my undivided attention now.

"What about them?"

"They don't match the attackers involved in William and Bella's case. They could have hired someone who still hasn't been named but as soon as the charges were doled out, they sang like canaries, naming anyone who would help reduce their sentence."

"Yeah, I agree. If they'd hired someone to trash Cassie's place, they would have been named and charged by now." My brows furrow, wondering who in the world would want to hurt Cassie. "Do any of the named accomplices have prints in the system?"

"Yes, they all have priors and have all been ruled out."

Fuck. "This is bad." I run a hand through my hair, tugging at the ends. A nervous habit that's seemed to make a reappearance as of late. "This means that whoever did that to her place is still out there."

Even though Cass and I aren't together anymore, that doesn't mean that I've stopped caring. Quite the contrary, now that I don't have her under my care, I'm even more worried about her day to day.

"And I'm guessing the prints you found don't match anything in the system either." It's not a question, more of a statement. Titus would have opened with the suspect's information, had he had it in the first place.

"Right-o." Titus nods, slapping the report onto my desk. "What do you want to do about it?"

"Doctors need to have their prints run, don't they? Find out if that's the case, and if so, see if they match a Woodrow Wilson."

Titus snickers. "Like the dead president?"

"Yes, only this one is very much alive and very much a creep."

Something in my gut tells me to pay the good doctor a visit. I'd bet my right nut Cass wouldn't appreciate the impromptu visit to her employer's office but I need to make sure she's safe.

If I happen to run into her then so be it.

I dial Becca's extension, "I need you to make me a rushed appointment with Dr. Woodrow Wilson. He has an office in Turtle Creek. See if he can get me in for a consult."

I've never considered plastic surgery before, but for Cass, I can pretend.

"Ren, what a pleasure seeing you again." Barbie is as pink as the scrunchie in her hair. "When your secretary called to make the appointment earlier, I knew I had to fit you right in. Although I must say that I'm surprised. There isn't a thing on you I'd ever change."

Batting her lashes, she purses her lips. For such a saccharine-sweet woman, she sure is forward.

"Nobody's perfect, Barbie." I wink, causing her to break into a fit of giggles.

I do my best to not look confused. There wasn't anything particularly funny about what I said, at least I don't think.

Wanting to get off the topic of my looks and on to anything else, I search the room for anything that could possibly come to my aid.

My eyes land on a framed picture of the petite Barbie with a massive Great Dane.

"What a gorgeous dog." I nod toward the frame. "Must be a handful to take care of though."

"Oh, this is Larkie Lark. And yes, he's such a ham. Loves to sit on my lap. To him, he's a teacup Yorkie." She rolls her eyes but smiles wide. *Mission accomplished.* "Maybe you could come over sometime. Seems like you'd be real good with dogs. Cassie tells me Bruce absolutely adores you."

My eyes narrow. I'm not sure if she's coming on to me, or if she's genuinely wanting to be friends.

"Ren." Dr. Wilson greets me from the doorway. "I thought I saw your name on my schedule today."

"Doctor. Yes, thank you for fitting me in on such short notice."

"That's all Barbie." He motions over to Barbie, who's been watching our conversation as if it were the most intense tennis match. "I didn't know until the appointment was in the books."

"Right. Well, thank you anyway." I begin walking forward. "Shall we get this over with?"

"Yes, of course." Dr. McCreeperson leads the way into an exam room. Once inside, he motions to the bed in the center. "Please take a seat."

Slapping on some gloves, he approaches me, raising both hands to my face, "May I?"

I nod, allowing him to inspect my face.

"So, rhinoplasty. The intake note said you wanted a consult on fixing a previously broken nose."

"Yes. Broke it playing soccer in college. I've had this bump ever since." I point toward the slight divot on the bridge of my nose. I honestly am okay with it—even think it adds character—but he doesn't have to know that.

"Yes, I see. Lucky for you, that's an easy fix." He pushes his lips to the side as if in contemplation. "However, any surgery where anesthesia is involved runs risks. Risks that include your inability to wake up from said surgery."

Did this asshole just threaten me? I think he did.

Cocking a brow, I take a dig, even though I have no right to. "That would make Cassie extremely unhappy, we wouldn't want that now, would we?"

I'm taking a chance on the fact that he has no idea Cassie and I aren't on talking terms. From the soured look on his face, I'd say it was a safe bet.

"So you and Cassie are still a thing..." He's not really asking, so I'm not going to dignify it with an answer. Besides, this gets me out of having to full-on lie. Something I hate doing.

"Why does that matter, Dr. Wilson? Do you have feelings for Cassie?" McCreepster's body stiffens and I wonder if it's for fear of confrontation or fear of getting caught.

The whole reason for this appointment was to dig deep and find out if this man possesses the gall to terrorize Cassie or if he's just another man, trapped in her web, forever orbiting the star that is Cassie.

His comment about my relationship with Cass gives me the perfect excuse, so I press further, seeing as he's not readily volunteering any information.

"Doc? Do you have romantic feelings toward Cass?"

"Why do I have the feeling that it was never your intention to seek my professional opinion about your nose?"

"That'd be because you're a smart man, Dr. Wilson. Despite your repeated failure to keep your hands to yourself, you still possess a brain." I cock a brow while jumping off the exam table.

"So, Doc. Out with it. Do you have feelings for Cassie? Feelings that extend beyond that of an employer-employee."

My six-foot-two meets his five-nine. The man is tough, I'll give him that. He's yet to back down and is standing his ground. Maybe he does have the balls to trash Cassie's place.

"I'd be careful if I were you, Ren. Would hate for your presumptions to get you into trouble." The man threatens me once more before taking two steps back and motioning toward the door. "Now if you'll excuse me, I have a list of patients that *do* actually want my professional services."

"I don't take kindly to threats, Woodie. Next time you issue one, be prepared to face the consequences." I close the door behind me quietly, not wanting to cause a scene.

There's no need to alarm Barbie or the other patients.

Finally back in my car, I dial Titus' number. "Brother, just left the doctor's office. Please tell me there was a match with the prints."

"Sorry, man. Still haven't received a copy of the report, but you'll be the first I call when I do."

I slam my hand down onto the steering wheel. *Fuck.* I need to find out who wrecked her place before they try something worse.

Even though the doctor didn't admit to anything, he gave me all sorts of crazy vibes. There's no doubt in my mind that he has what it takes to be a stalker. Cassie's stalker.

"Okay. I appreciate it. For now, I'd like to have someone tailing the doctor. Put any of the charges on my personal card. I'll be handling the invoices for Cassie's case." I scrub my face with my hand, knowing she isn't going to like having someone tailing her either. "Also get a detail on Cassie again. And have them fly under the radar. I don't want her alerted to their presence."

"You sure that's such a good idea? Last time you tried taking charge of her free will, she ended up pissed and locked in a car."

Visions of a fiery Cassie has my dick twitching in my pants. Closing my eyes, I let out the breath I'd been holding, "Just do it. When it comes to her safety, she doesn't get a say."

"Ten-four, brother." Titus' chuckle fades as he pulls the phone away and cuts the line.

He can laugh all he wants, but the day he falls in love, he'll be the one acting a fool and putting aside all logic and reason.

Love. That's what this is. There's no doubt in my mind that I love that woman with every bit of my fucked-up heart.

From the moment at the bar in Uptown, I was drawn to her light. Something in me recognized her. *My little angel.*

The fire in her kept me coming back for more, but it wasn't until that moment at the tree where it all came together.

I'd just been released from Lew Sterret, after posting bail for charges of public intoxication. So of course the logical thing to do would be to stop by the liquor store to get more booze.

Somehow I found my way to the tree. The tree that would lead me to Cassie, my little angel.

I shake my head. God, she must have thought I was a fucking mess. And truth be told, I was. The night before I'd found out our mom had taken her life.

After a long battle with depression, she decided she'd set herself free.

ELEANOR ALDRICK

My eyes squeeze shut, a lone tear falling down my cheek. After all this time, I still don't understand. I'm a mixture of emotions, all previously suppressed, locked up, and hidden away. But somehow Cassie has managed to unearth each and every one, bringing them out to play and wreak havoc with my emotional state.

Rage flows, burning me from the inside. *How could a mother leave her children behind. Didn't she love us enough? Weren't we enough for her?*

As soon as the words run rampant in my mind, I immediately feel a pang of guilt. *Fuck, Ren. She was sick.*

There wasn't a memory of hers that isn't tainted with the bitter reality of her sickness. Her laughter and hugs, whenever she doled them out, were never whole.

It was always as if something were missing. Like she was putting on a show, a facade, the emotion never truly reaching her.

Superficial. All the joy we felt, it was all superficial.

Cassie was right. Wherever she was now, at least she was free of the illness. The only solace to my misery, that she'd finally be free of her sorrow.

The irony isn't lost on me that she'd lost her own but somehow managed to leave behind a shiny new supply for Aiden and me.

And man, was that sorrow deep. It cut me open and wrung me dry. The only reprieve came from that one little angel. She's the one who helped me find my peace.

How twisted is it that the little girl who helped me heal would be the same woman who tore me down over a decade later. *Fate is one twisted motherfucker.*

There's probably some lesson in there somewhere but my soul is tired and all I want to do is what I know. What I've always done to take away the sting of reality.

Occupy every waking hour with work, leaving no room for thought or emotion as it pertains to my shattered heart.

Picking up my phone once more, I dial the office.

"Becca, get the jet ready. I'm heading back to California."

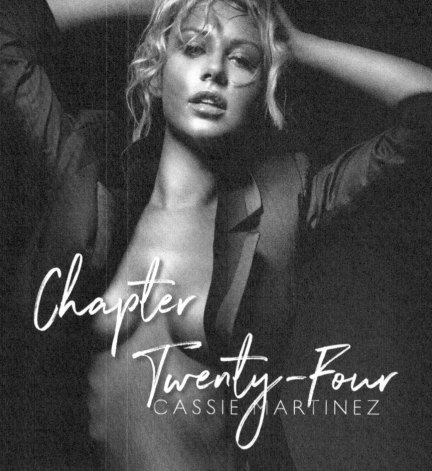

Chapter Twenty-Four
CASSIE MARTINEZ

I T'S THE THIRD MONTH since I walked out of Ren's penthouse apartment and not a day goes by that I don't kick myself in the ass.

I should've stayed. Demanded an explanation. Sure, I'd just served him his broken heart on a platter the night before, but I was there to apologize. Things were supposed to get better, not worse, dammit.

"Are you done in there?" Carmen bangs on the door to her tiny bathroom. Mind you, it's the only bathroom in her two-bedroom home.

I know I shouldn't be crashing at her place when she already lives with her husband and five kids in a five hundred square foot home.

Okay, so maybe I'm exaggerating a little on the square footage, but it seriously cramped, and I'm a shitty sister for adding to the shortage of space.

"I'm out." I open the door and step into the narrow hallway, motioning toward the interior of the outdated bathroom, complete with wall to wall pink tile.

She rolls her eyes while stepping in, "You're lucky I love your difficult ass. I just needed to get the kids' detangler." She grabs something from under the sink before hooking my arm in hers and walking us toward the living room. "Sit with me. It's time we have this talk."

I groan loudly, dreading the inevitable. She's been extremely patient, never questioning my reasoning as to why I've decided to camp both Bruce and me in her home.

"Cassandra, you know I love you with all my heart, but I'm your older sister. And with that position comes great responsibility. Like tough love."

I roll in my lips, knowing where this is going. "I'm sorry I've invaded your home. But think of the bright side, this way you don't have to buy the kids a dog. They can just play with Bruce and I'm the one who has to care for him, not you." I shoot her my most convincing smile before continuing. "Besides, you know that I couldn't stay at Mom's, not with Dad being back. I can't stand the man and living under the same roof as them is just asking for trouble."

"Cass, this isn't about you staying here. You know we will

always make room for family." She plops my three-year-old niece on her lap and begins to brush her wind-blown hair, no doubt a mess from having been running around in the back yard with her older sisters and Bruce. "This is about *the reason* behind your staying here. I know you have a perfectly good apartment you're still paying for. Why haven't you gone back to staying at your place? Isn't it safe now that they've caught Bella's attackers?"

I pick at my nails, unable to look at her eyes.

"Yes. I just can't. Everything there reminds me of him." My chest constricts and I feel like I'm running out of air again. My panic attacks have been increasing ever since the night Ren asked me to marry him and I fucked everything up.

"Oh, Cass. I'm sorry. Is there any way you two could patch things up?" Her eyes are warm, holding concern only someone who's loved and lost could truly understand. "You know, Hernando and I have had really bad fights before, but we always find a way to come back to one another. That's how you know it's true love. When time and space don't heal your sorrow, but instead it evolves into a growing need." She puts her baby down and grabs both of my hands squeezing them. "The fact that it's been three months and you still look just as gutted, if not worse, tells me there's something deeper here. Something worth taking a chance on."

I can't look her in the eyes. I know if I do, the floodgates will open and I'll start sobbing yet again. The tears haven't really stopped since messing things up with Ren. They've just become more private. Instead of openly weeping, I wait until everyone's tucked away in their rooms and Bruce is the only one there to bear witness.

"Did you hear me, little sis?" Carmen brings up one hand to my chin, lifting my face to hers and giving me no choice but to look at her head-on.

"Yessssss. I heard you, Carmen." I bite my lower lip, trying to inflict pain in a miserable attempt to keep the tears at bay. "Is it worth it?"

"Is what worth it?"

"All the fights, the going back and forth with your man, losing yourself to him, to your children... I never see you do anything for yourself. It's like you've turned into this alternate version of Mom." I shift my gaze to the wall, feeling like an ass for even saying all this but I really need to know. "A big part of why I messed things up with Ren that night was because I didn't want to turn into Mom."

Carmen laughs, "You didn't want to turn into me either, based on what you're saying." She pats my shoulder and looks at me like she... *pities me*? "Oh, girl. You have no idea what blessings true love brings, do you?"

I just sit there confused as hell. Why is she laughing? I'd be offended, angry even, if I were in her shoes.

"No, you don't. Because you've always kept that heart of yours well guarded against all men. Well, until Ren." She shakes her head side to side as her expression grows serious. "There is no greater honor than to be a mother to my children or the other half to my man. And do you know why that is, Cass?"

I must look as confused as I feel because she continues without my having to say a word.

"Because when you find the perfect partner in life, and you're brave enough to give yourself to them completely, they treasure you. Treasure every bit of what you're willing to share and not only do they revel in your love, but they also give themselves back to you tenfold." Her smile lights up her face, making her love palpable. "And the beauty of that is, it makes you want to give more of yourself, because you aren't really losing if you're gaining so much more. You see, the cycle keeps going and that love just keeps growing and growing. It's pure magic."

Magic. Oh, how I've felt the beginning of that magic myself. And *it is* beautiful.

Carmen takes my hand and pats it. "That, my sister, is the difference between choosing the right and wrong man. From what I've heard and seen, I think Ren could be the right man."

I'm a full-blown weeping mess at this point. Even if my sister is right, and Ren is the perfect partner for me, how in the world am I going to fix what I've done wrong?

Carmen wipes away at my face. "Psst. Are you going to get that?"

She nods toward my bag which is now vibrating on the coffee table. Taking my phone out, I see that it's William's number. Wondering why he's calling instead of Bella, I pick up immediately. "William, is Bella okay?"

"Hey, Cass." He laughs into the phone. "Sorry to bother you, I know I don't usually call. Bella is fine but I have a massive favor to ask of you."

Color me curious because I'm dying to find out what would make this man call *me*. He's always kept to himself, and aside from helping sit for Harper every now and then, our interactions have been minimal. Especially after he broke Bella's heart with that unnecessary breakup over the summer.

"I sort of need you in Boston tomorrow. Well, The Cape to be exact. I'm proposing the Bella and I want everyone who's important to us present."

My heart begins to beat overtime. "Oh my god!" I squeal into the phone. "This is so exciting!" My excitement is cut short when the next words to fly out of his mouth hit my eardrums.

"Great! Ren is in California but he'll be taking the jet back to Dallas to pick up everyone else. I'm hoping you can meet them at the private airstrip tonight."

My heart stops and I swear the room is spinning. Either I have a serious case of vertigo or my emotions are wreaking havoc on me once more.

"I thought you said you didn't need me there until tomorrow? I can just catch a commercial flight there in the morning. No big deal."

"Well, the thing is I'm proposing at sunrise and there aren't any commercial flights that could get you there in time. Besides, if you tried to book a redeye flight for tonight, it would cost you a small fortune." There's a long pause before he resumes speaking. "Is there a reason you don't want to be on the jet tonight?"

Not wanting to give anything away as it pertains to Ren and me, I quickly jump in and shoot that theory down. "No, none at all. I just hadn't had time to pack or prepare Bruce for a stay without me."

My sister who's been standing a couple of feet away this entire time rolls her eyes while flinging a kitchen towel at me.

"Okay, I will be there. Just text me the details and I'll make it happen. Do you need me to bring anything?"

"Just yourself. I know Bella would really appreciate having her best friend present. Thanks again, and see you tomorrow."

"See you tomorrow."

I guess I'm seeing Ren sooner rather than later.

ACTS OF SALVATION

"Soooo, are you going to tell me what that was all about?" My sister smirks while narrowing her eyes.

"William is proposing to Bella tomorrow and he wants me there." I stand there, staring at her blankly, still not fully having let that sink in.

"Must be something in the air. Didn't Ren just propose to you a couple of months ago? Hopefully, Bella handles it better than you did." I know this is her version of tough love, but man does that dig burn.

My mouth is hanging open, "Carmen, that was low."

"Just calling it like I see it." She gives me a warm smile as she pours me a glass of wine. "So, does this mean you'll be seeing Ren? This could be your chance to make things right."

I take a sip of the red, letting the richness of its flavor play across my tongue. "Thank you for the liquid courage because it looks like I'll be needing it. They're out in Cape Cod right now so he wants me to fly on their private jet tonight. It's a sunrise proposal and there aren't any commercial flights open that would get me there in time. Well, none that wouldn't cost me my savings."

"Ummm." Carmen smacks me upside the head. "Why in the world would you pass up flying on a private jet?" Her eyes narrow as a knowing grin spreads across her lips. "Ahhhh, Ren will be on it, won't he?"

I lift my eyes to hers and take another sip before replying, "Ding, ding, ding."

Carmen gently nudges me off of the bar stool I'd been sitting on. "What are you doing still sitting here? You need to be packing and getting yourself all dolled up. You have a man to win over."

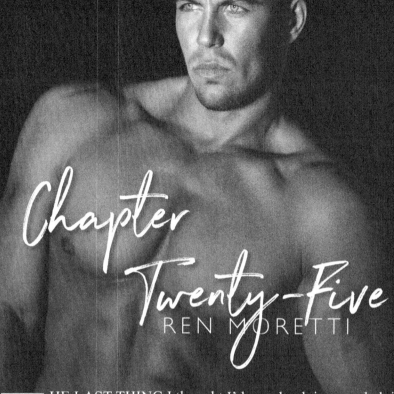

Chapter Twenty-Five
REN MORETTI

THE LAST THING I thought I'd ever be doing was helping my best friend propose to my niece.

But here I am. On the firm jet, flying from California to Texas and then out to the east coast where I have to spring my nephews out of boarding school and then drive them over at the ass-crack of dawn to the Cape.

I mean, proposing at sunrise in the Cape is a hell of a lot better than proposing to the girl you love under a tree... at a gas station... fifty feet from a dumpster.

I run a hand across my face. *Fuck*. No wonder Cass freaked

out. I knew she was skittish as hell and then I have to go and pull an asshat move like proposing in the worst possible location.

Speaking of Cass, William mentioned she agreed to meet the rest of the crew at the hanger. I'd be lying if I said I wasn't excited.

"Would you like another drink before we land, sir? We're about to descend," the flight attendant interrupts my thoughts of Cass, adding to my annoyance.

"No, thank you." I drink the last bit of Jack and hand her the tumbler before returning my attention to the window—back to thoughts of Cassie.

Little angel, have you missed me as much as I've missed you?

My stomach knots and I'm not sure if it's the change in cabin pressure or if it's the impending meetup with the woman who built me up only to tear me down.

The wheels unfurl before making contact with the asphalt of the runway, bringing me that much closer to an answer.

No matter what happens on this trip, I have every intention of finding out what possessed Cass to cut me off as if I didn't mean a thing to her.

Regardless of how shitty my proposal was, I didn't deserve the cold shoulder she served me with.

I must've been lost in my thoughts longer than I thought because the cabin door is lowering and I immediately hear Titus and Hudson arguing over a bet they've placed.

The first one to cross the threshold is Ashley, William's sister, toting the now two-year-old Harper, her adorable pigtails swinging side to side as Ashley bounces her on her hip.

"Hey, how was the flight from Cali?" Ashley asks as she places Harper down on one of the captain chairs.

"Uneventful." I give her a quick smile. I don't mean to sound like an ass but there's only one thing on my mind and she's stepping into the cabin this very moment.

My eyes rove over every inch of her. *God, she's a sight to behold.* Wearing a jersey maxi dress and wedged heels, the woman looks like something straight out of a magazine.

She must feel my burning stare because her eyes find mine and there's no doubt that she feels the electricity charging between us.

"Cass." I greet her with a lone nod, trying to keep my expression neutral.

Surprising the hell out of me, she struts my way, seating herself next to me. It's clear I'm unable to hide my reaction because she softly giggles.

"Hey, Ren." She smiles and it's as if all the crap I'd been thinking before vanishes in a puff of smoke. "You're looking good." Her cheeks flush, and I wonder if I've stroked out or something.

My brows come together, and my mouth is slightly agape. She's acting as if things are gravy between us, but last I remember, she took Bruce from our place without even saying goodbye and then sent someone to pick up the rest of her things so she wouldn't have to see me.

"I'm sorry, did I miss something?" Hudson interrupts our intense stare-off. "Because from where I'm standing, the tension between you two would suggest there's been a lot going on that wasn't shared with the team."

"Quit it, Hud." Titus attempts to rein in the instigator of our motley crew.

I love my friends as if they were my own flesh and blood, but sometimes they can be such a pain in the ass. *Like now.*

"What? I was simply making an observation. It's not like everyone hadn't noticed it. I was just stating what everyone else was thinking, out loud."

"Hudson, you were being rude." Ashley arches a brow, and though I'm grateful for her backing me up, I know she's just put herself directly in Hudson's line of fire.

"I don't think you want to jump in on this, sweetheart. I've noticed the looks you and Titus have been giving each other."

Titus stands, getting directly in the path between Ashley and Hudson. "I suggest you keep your comments to yourself or I'll personally see to it that the stint you just did in Bumfuck Arkansas becomes a permanent post for you."

I chuckle, knowing how much Hudson hated being on that job. He'd let us know through our group email *at least* once a day.

Taking Titus' threat seriously, because the man does not kid, Hudson finally calms his ass down and zips his trap.

Looking back toward Cass, I see that her cheeks are flushed. No doubt she's probably embarrassed from being called out by Hudson. I take her hand in mine and gently squeeze. "You okay?"

She brushes her thumb back and forth against my fingers, the sensation sending a direct jolt to my cock.

Down boy, now is not the time.

"Much better now, thank you." She smiles coyly at me as my own eyes widen a little in surprise.

Not only is she okay with me touching her but she's touching me back *and* flirting. I must be in some sort of alternate reality.

"Cass, are you feeling well?" I don't want to come off as unappreciative of her affection but I'm genuinely confused.

"Yes." A look that could be read as contrite flashes across

Cassie's face. "I was hoping we could talk at some point during this trip."

Fuck yes, we can talk. We can do all the talking you want. I'm tempted to carry her into the jet's bedroom but that would definitely send Hudson into a tailspin. "Of course. Maybe you can join me on my trip to pick up the boys later tonight."

"I'd like that. I'd like that a lot." Cassie blushes before withdrawing her hand from mine and pulling out a book from her bag.

I pull out my phone and try to focus on emails, a vain attempt at distracting myself from what just transpired, but it's pointless. No matter what I do, nothing will detract from the fact that this is going to be one *very* long flight.

I sit behind the wheel of the Escalade I've rented to take us to New Hampshire, where the boys are in boarding school thanks to my brother's recent freakout. He hasn't been the same since his brain injury and even though I wish the twins were living close to family, I think that for now, this is what's best.

"I take it Aiden doesn't know you're picking up the boys?" Cassie looks at me with amusement dancing in her eyes.

"Bingo." I point a finger at her and wink. Being playful with her like this just feels right. Setting my resolve, I decide this needs to be our new norm and I'll stop at nothing to make it happen.

ELEANOR ALDRICK

"Disowning Bella and cutting her out of the boy's lives was wrong, and he should know better than to think that I'd stand by him. Thankfully for William and Bella, I'm an appointed guardian in their school's release forms."

"I really hope your brother comes around. It would be a shame for him to miss out on more of Bella's life just because he's being bull-headed."

We stop at a red light before getting onto the highway, looking over at Cassie, I can't hold back any longer. Placing a hand behind her neck, I pull her face to mine, depositing a bruising kiss where teeth clash and tongues tangle in a desperate attempt at being closer.

On the same wavelength, Cass unbuckles her seatbelt, crosses over the center console, and straddles me in the driver's seat.

Her hands dig through my hair as she brings our faces together. "I've missed you."

Needing no further invitation, my hands slide underneath her dress, pulling it off in one fell swoop. I press her bare chest to mine, kissing her lips, her chin, her neck—trailing my way down to the most beautiful pair of tits I've ever seen before taking one into my mouth and suckling it like a man starving.

Cass arches her back, grinding herself onto my erection and moaning my name as if it were a prayer.

I'm so hard, my dick has made an appearance at the top of my trousers, begging for its release. As if reading my mind, Cass set's me free before sliding her panties to the side and lowering herself onto me.

Fuuuuuck. I was not expecting that, and it takes everything in me not to come right then and there.

Somewhere in the background, I can hear a horn honking, but

ACTS OF SALVATION

I'm too far gone in Cassie to care.

I grab her hips and rock her into me, creating a rhythm only we understand. With every push and pull we tell a story. A story of missed moments and apologies, tears and sorrow—but most importantly, a story of love.

Our eyes lock and in that moment, I'm back home. Where I belong.

Our frenzied movements are fast and furious, needing to get deeper, closer—seeking that moment where our bodies and soul become one.

I don't think I could ever get enough of this.

With a shuddering breath, we climax together, hanging on as if we were each other's life raft. And to be honest, in this moment, that's what she is. My tether to a life worth living.

"I'm sorry." Cass goes to move off of me but I anchor her down with both hands on her hips.

"Don't move." With one hand still firmly gripped on her, I maneuver the car off to the side of the road. "Now, tell me why you're sorry."

"For jumping you like that. I swear I haven't been with anyone since us. I'm clean." She looks away as if pained.

Pulling her face back to mine, I tell her the truth. "Neither have I."

The look of shock that registers on her face has me furrowing my brows.

"But what about Becca?"

"What about Becca?" She looks about as confused as I am. "Did she say something to you that would make you think I'd been with someone else?"

"She didn't have to say a damn thing. The fact that she was topless in your kitchen while you showered in the other room spoke volumes." Cassie attempts to remove herself from my lap but I'm not letting her go that easily.

"Ohhhhh no you don't. You don't get to jump off after that bomb you just dropped." The pieces start coming together, slowly but surely. "The day you picked up Bruce. Is that when you happened to find Becca?"

Cass nods. She must be fuming since she can't even form words.

"She'd been by to drop off a file for me, I was about to fly to California on an assignment. She's always had a key to my place since she waters my plants when I'm out of town." Cass' eyes narrow at this revelation, but I'm just getting started. "When I'd come out of the shower, she looked a bit disheveled but I didn't think anything of it. Especially when she told me you'd just been by to pick up Bruce and didn't want to see me or say goodbye. After that bit of news, the last thing on my mind was the appearance of her top."

Cass' mouth is hanging wide open. "That fucking bitch. I'm gonna make her pay..."

"Don't. Leave this one to me. She crossed a line when she fucked with the woman I love."

Cass' eyes sparkle and a tear escapes the corner of her eye. Bringing her face closer, I kiss it away. "Shhhh, baby. I can't stand to see you cry."

I'm still holding her head against mine when I hear it.

"I love you too," her words come out so low they're barely audible, but they're there, out in the open.

ACTS OF SALVATION

My chest swells, wanting to drown in them—reveling in the three consonants, four vowels, and one indisputable meaning. "You have no idea how long I've wanted to hear those words." I kiss her forehead before pulling her away. "And we're still not done talking. But right now we need to move this car off the shoulder and get back on the road."

Cassie laughs as she crawls over the console and back onto her seat. "Hey, at least we didn't get arrested for public indecency."

A chuckle escapes me and it feels so damn good to be this light and carefree again. "Yea, but it'd totally be worth it if we did."

Chapter Twenty-Six
CASSIE MARTINEZ

THE PAST TEN HOURS have been insane. It was a mad dash to get to the boys' boarding school before the front office closed for the day, and once we were there, it practically took a visit from the pope himself to have the twins be released in our care.

Granted, it's nice to know the kids are cared for when they're at school, but given the fact that Ren is listed as a guardian with the ability to withdraw them if necessary, it all seemed like a bit of overkill.

If you ask me, the prep school screamed more of 'upscale

penitentiary' than learning institution.

By the time we got into the Cape, it was a little past midnight. I helped Ren get the boys settled in their room and ended up passing out myself during story time. It was the cutest thing ever. Since we didn't have any books with us, Ren made up an impromptu fairy tale involving a princess and a magical tree.

I'm not gonna lie, seeing him with the boys stirred something inside me, waking up a maternal clock I didn't even know I possessed.

Adding to the swoon-worthiness, Ren carried me to his bed and let me sleep in, only waking me up when it was absolutely necessary. Given the fact that William is proposing at sunrise, it's at the ass-crack of dawn, but still...every minute counts when it comes to sleep.

Especially when I've been charged with keeping the boys out of trouble until the proposal. I'm pulling both twins' hands, trying to keep them behind the small hedge of shrubbery lining William and Bella's vacation rental.

I know with certainty that if I weren't holding on to them they'd have blown the surprise by now.

"My sweet Isabella. If you could only see what I see. You are more than enough. You are everything, and if you let me, I will spend the rest of my life showing you how worthy you are." William shifts, dropping his arm from Bella's side. "Open your eyes, baby."

He's dropped down onto one knee and in his right hand is a small box.

"Yes. *Oh my fucking god, yes!*" Bella jumps on William, depositing endless kisses onto his face. "How? How are you so perfect?"

ACTS OF SALVATION

"I didn't even ask the question yet. I had a whole speech prepared." William chuckles.

"You can tell me later after you fuck me senseless. This calls for celebratory sex!"

I bite my lip, trying to stifle a laugh. Ren's been recording this whole time and I'm surprised he's managed to stay quiet. It can't be easy seeing his baby niece getting proposed to by his best friend. Especially not with that exceptionally colorful commentary.

Clearing his throat, Ren finally chimes in. "Well, this is going to make a great story for the grandkids."

The boys—seeing Ren's comment as their cue to party—beeline it straight to Bella, snickering the whole way there.

"Oh my god. When did y'all get here?" Bella wipes her tears away.

"We flew in on the jet last night." I shoot her a salacious smile while popping open the bottle of champagne I'd brought with me. "How about you come inside and we settle for celebratory mimosas instead of the sex, at least until we've all cleared out?"

"Yes. Of course. You guys realize I had no idea you were here, right?" Her cheeks redden as she brings her hands to her face.

The boys—not having any of it—tug at Bella's hands, exposing her face.

"You said *fucking!*" Matt singsongs before both boys bust into a fit of giggles.

Bella pulls them into a tight embrace. "How did you two get here?"

"I picked them up from New Hampshire last night. I'm their emergency pickup, and this definitely qualifies as an emergency. It's not every day we see a grown man propose to a teenager." Ren is quick to answer, and it's not lost on me that I was omitted from this telling of events.

To be honest, I'm not sure if I should feel offended or relieved. *Maybe a bit of both?*

First, he didn't mention my going to pick up the boys. And second, didn't he just propose *to me*? I'm nineteen and technically still a teenager. My head spins at what that could possibly mean.

*Does he regret asking m*e?

"*Fuck you.*" William's cursing pulls me out of my thoughts. Looking toward him, I see him shove at Ren. "You're just jealous I found my forever and you're still out there playing the field with nothing to show for it."

Unable to help myself, my eyes seek out Ren's. In that one split second, our eyes connect, sharing a million questions.

Needing some air, I quickly slip away and head toward the front of the cottage. I need to pull myself together. I didn't come this far with Ren just to throw in the towel at the first sign of trouble. So what if he didn't mention me to Bella? Now is hardly the time, given the current state of celebration.

I'm about to sit myself down on the entryway bench when I notice a form making its way up the path to the home.

Oh my god.

I rush to open the door, refusing to let this man ruin Bella's special day. Standing my full five-foot-two, I cross my arms, barring his entry.

Aiden, Bella's dad, gives me a contrite smile. "Cassie, hi."

"Aiden." I don't budge, nor do I reward him with a smile. The way he kicked Bella out after all she sacrificed for him makes him one of my least favorite people. *Ever.*

ACTS OF SALVATION

Holding up his hands in a placating gesture, he moves a step back. "Look, I'm not here to cause any trouble. I figured everyone would be here after the jet landed at Chatham Air Field."

I narrow my eyes at him. "Okay, so you knew the jet was here... but how'd you know *who'd* be here?"

He gives me an uneasy smile. "I'm a Navy SEAL, Cass. Not much I can't figure out."

I'm not amused. Seeing that I'm not budging, he hits me with an emotional one-two I can't refuse.

"Look. I messed up with Bella, and not just recently. A lot of soul searching led me to see how I failed her as a father. She continuously gave herself to me and I selfishly took. Never worrying about what she needed. I've wasted precious time with my only daughter. Please, Cass. Don't let me waste another second without righting things with her."

Gut. Punched. I'm a girl with daddy issues. There's no way I'd deny him entry after that speech. As soon as he poured his heart out to me and admitted to being in the wrong, I was a goner.

Bella deserves a chance to have a good relationship with her only remaining parent. I'm definitely not going to stand in the way of that if what this man is saying is true.

Finally breaking my stance, I step aside and motion him in, but not before issuing a warning. "Navy SEAL or not, if you hurt her one more time, I'll personally see to it that you never see her again."

Walking into the home as if he's been here before, he gives me a warm smile and nods in agreement.

I let him walk ahead, not ready to join the group just yet. I'm about to sit on the bench again when a strong set of hands wrap around me from behind. Melting back into his chest, I breathe his scent in. *Ren.*

"Little angel. Why'd you run off?"

His words are like a soft caress, sending shivers rippling across my skin. I close my eyes, wanting to live in this moment forever. In his arms, nothing can harm me. I'm invincible.

His lips on my neck have my eyes shooting open. "*Ren.* What if someone sees?"

"Let them." He continues to trail kisses onto the top of my shoulders.

"But if you don't care, then why'd you omit that I went with you to pick up the boys?" I turn in his arms, needing to see his face.

He's grinning wide. "You can't possibly think I'd want to hide you?" He takes my face in both his hands and kisses my lips. "I didn't want to hide you Cass, I just didn't want to break into William and Bella's big moment with a big announcement like ours."

"Oh, yeah? And what announcement would that be?" I bite the corner of my lower lip, trying not to smile.

"That we're in love." Ren waggles his brows playfully. "And that you're officially moving in with me."

My jaw drops as I look up into those gorgeous eyes of his. He's dead serious. Not a hint of amusement to be found. "*What?*"

"You heard me." He turns me, slapping my ass before gently pushing me toward the living area where everyone else is gathered. "We can hash out the details on the flight home. Apparently, the rest of the crew is staying on the Cape for the weekend."

"And what if I wanted to stay and party too?" I turn to look at him, offering a teasing glare.

"You can't. You're going to be too busy moving into your new home."

ACTS OF SALVATION

I shake my head, unable to say another word as we rejoin the celebration. Heading toward Bella, I look back at him one more time.

This is far from over, buddy.

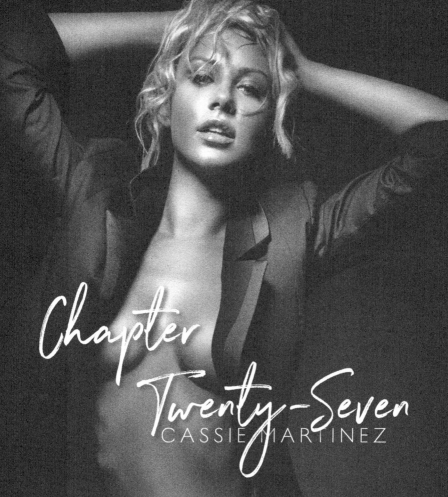

Chapter Twenty-Seven
CASSIE MARTINEZ

I DON'T THINK I'LL EVER get used to being in one of these. Flying private *definitely* has its perks. My hand traces the supple leather of the seat I'm in, in awe of its craftsmanship. It's so buttery soft I want to rip off my dress and rub against it like a cat in heat.

"Do you like it?"

Looking up, I see the intensity in Ren's eyes. Unable to formulate words, I simply nod.

"This is where you belong, Cass. You're so precious, you deserve to be surrounded by nothing but the best." Ren grabs me by the hips, pulling me onto his lap, my legs straddling either side of him. "With me, you'll never want for anything. I promise."

Our lips brush together, and my incessant inner dialogue can't help but ruin the moment. "What's the catch?"

At my words, Ren freezes, pulling away from my lips. His eyes are squinty, making him look boyish if that's even possible. "What makes you think that there's a catch? I want to take care of you, Cass. Give you a home. Make you happy. Make you mine."

"But I already have a home." My words are like a slap to his face, and immediately I know I need to rectify my wrong. "What I mean is... why is it so important for me to live with you?"

If I were being completely honest with myself, I'd let him know that it was the whole control issue that scares the shit out of me.

Fuck it. Here goes nothing.

"Look, my dad has always controlled my mom. He wouldn't even let her go to night school." I shake my head, knowing I probably sound like a damaged nut case, listing the transgressions of another man completely unrelated to the one sitting before me. "When you do things like tell me what I can and can't do, it freaks me out. It makes me think you're trying to control me."

I feel Ren's body soften from its previously tense state. "Cassie, this should go without saying, but I am *not* your father. If I ever make a decision as far as you're concerned, it's because I want what's best for you—not what's best for me. It doesn't come from a selfish place." He strokes my hair, placing a soft kiss on my forehead. "The reason why I want you to move in is because it's safer at my place. I can keep a closer eye on you, especially since we still don't know who broke into your place and trashed it."

My heart picks up its pace tenfold. "What did you just say? I thought they caught the people who were harassing Bella." *I'm truly confused, how did I not know this?* "When did you find this out?"

Ren tightens his grip on my hips. "Right after you left me."

My chest aches at the memory, but a couple of seconds later his words finally register. *He's known for months!*

No doubt his words were chosen with care because my first instinct would've been to jump off his lap for such an omission. But the reminder that I shattered his heart for doing the same thing I almost did again, helps keep me in check, toeing the line from sanity to insanity.

Taking in a centering breath, I gently let him have it. "You can't keep those types of things from me, Ren. If we're going to work, you need to include me on anything that involves my health and well-being. What if I'd been attacked because I didn't know to be on the lookout?"

"You should always be vigilant. You're a beautiful woman, little angel, and there are some very sick people in this world." Ren runs his hand up my back, weaving his fingers into my hair and softly pulling. "But that's a moot point now. You're mine, and I take care of what's mine."

His declaration of possession should scare the shit out of me but I can't help but glow, basking in the light of his love. *I am his and he is mine.*

"Okay, so that resolves my moving in with you."

Ren takes his free hand and runs it up my ribcage, stopping just below my breast, his thumb gently caressing its underside and making me audibly gasp.

"Mhmmm." Ren moves his hand up a little, letting his thumb flick my hardened nipple over the material of my sundress.

So distracting. I find myself slowly rocking back and forth over the bulge in his jeans. "Wha- What about the job situation? You told me to quit. What was your excuse then?"

I'm half listening, half reveling in the sensation of his cock applying pressure to my clit.

"Hmm? Oh, I thought you didn't want to work for the douche. Didn't he cross the line on multiple occasions?"

"Okay, so you've got a point there too..." I nip at his lip and he groans. "But next time, instead of telling, try asking."

"Bite me like that again and I'll ask you anything you want." Ren places both of his hands on my ass, lifting us both from the seat and carrying us toward the rear of the plane.

"Where are we going?"

"To bed. I'm not keen on sharing what's mine with the flight crew."

My eyes go wide with surprise. "There's a bed?"

"Yes, and before you ask. You're the first."

I bury my face in his neck, trying to hide my reddening complexion. "How'd you know what I was thinking?"

"What can I say, I know my little angel." Ren pushes on a panel, the secret door exposing a small yet comfortable room with a large bed to the right.

Without warning, Ren flings me onto the bed, eliciting a squeal from me. *Oh, yes.* If he wants rough, I'll give him rough.

I wrap my legs around his waist and bring him down onto the bed, rolling him over just before impact with the mattress. Ripping open his white dress shirt, I scrape my nails down his chest and onto his abs. The red trails of possession marking him as mine.

I lick the indents of his delicious washboard abs, complete with that panty-melting 'V' leading me straight to the most impressive cock I've ever seen or felt. A quick glance up lets me know that tongue session wiped the smirk right off his face. *Much better.*

Hunger. His eyes burn with it, consuming him to the point where the muscle in his jaw tics as he anticipates my next move.

"Baby, if you don't do something quick, I'm bound to rip that little dress right off and have my way with you. Fuck the foreplay."

My chest rumbles with laughter. He wants me as bad as I want him. *Good.*

I unbuckle his belt, sliding it out of the loops with one smooth jerk, eliciting the most satisfying sound. *Woosh.*

Giving Ren a sultry smile, I fold the leather in two and snap it taut.

My stomach flutters at the vision before me. This typically groomed man, all disheveled and ready to play.

Upping the ante, Ren bites his juicy bottom lip—our smoldering eyes connecting and sharing a thousand words with that one glance.

Unable to hold back any longer, I lower myself onto him and trail the material of the leather along his side. Grabbing both of his hands, I secure them with the belt positioned above his head and take his mouth—my tongue urgently seeking its other half.

"*Mine,*" I whisper into him.

"*Yours,*" he breathes into me.

A single tear rolls down my face as I realize the gift this man has just given me. Here he is, the epitome of domineering. An alpha male to the max, and he's given me full control over him. He's laid his heart out on the line time and time again, and to top it all off, here he lies in a vulnerable position, declaring himself as mine.

All of the things I've feared would be my downfall when it came to Ren are the opposite. They are blessings and letting myself have them boils down to one word. *Control.*

Ren possesses an inordinate amount of wealth, and if I were being honest, that scared the shit out of me.

The reason why I despise the wealthy isn't because of the money itself, but because of the power and control it affords them. They lord it over like power-hungry fiends, callous toward those beneath them.

I'd seen this repeatedly throughout my childhood as my mother waited tables, served as a hotel cleaning lady, and later in life, a nanny—almost every one of her employers exuded these horrible traits. Given the opportunity, they would exploit those beneath them, using their money as the proverbial whip and demand unabashed control.

Pair my disdain for wealthy people and a man who's favorite pastime is telling me what to do, and it's no wonder I was running for the hills. But no more. Looking back at all of his actions, I see the truth. Everything he's done, it's been for me. To protect me. To make me happy.

Sure, he's bossy, but his actions are never selfish. He always puts me first and it's about damn time I showed him the same.

Lowering myself between his legs, I wrap both of my hands around his magnificent cock, licking the salty bead of precum off the tip.

"Mmmmm. Delicious." I lick my lips as Ren releases a hiss, a mixture of pleasure and agony.

Slowly but firmly I begin to stroke the velvety skin of his shaft up and down in a rhythmic motion, reveling in how his hips buck with every pass.

"Angel, please. Suck my cock and put me out of my misery."

His words have me giving him a sensuous grin. Darting my tongue out, I lap at the warm red head before finally putting him out of his misery and taking him fully into my mouth.

Hollowing out my mouth, I suck him in deep, savoring the musky taste that's all him.

Ren releases a feral growl as I take him in deeper, the tip of his thick cock touching the back of my throat. He bucks into me but stops himself, letting me be the one in control. *God, I love this man.*

Rewarding him, I swallow even deeper, never ceasing my circular stroking up and down his lengthy shaft.

"*Fuuuuuck.* I'm about to blow, baby."

I withdraw my mouth immediately, the look of shock on his face quickly replaced with one of ecstasy as I lower my pussy down onto his cock, pumping myself up and down while grinding on his root each time there's friction.

"God, you're beautiful like this." Ren's ravenous eyes rove over every inch of my exposed flesh, his mouth opening wide with every roll of our hips.

Our sweaty bodies create the most delicious sounds as our pace becomes urgent.

Meeting me thrust for thrust, I lift both hands toward Ren's head, running my fingers through his thick hair and pulling.

Reaching his face forward, he takes one of my breasts into his mouth suckling and biting at the nipple.

And that's it. That's all it takes. I'm spiraling down the biggest climax my short nineteen years have ever gifted me with.

As soon as his massive erection slid into my wet channel, I

stood no chance. My body was primed to within an inch of itself and all it took to make me unravel was this sexy man's mouth on my nipple, the sensation of which shot straight down to my clit, exploding every single nerve ending in my body.

With a violent shudder, I contract and release over and over, the sensation driving Ren to his breaking point and causing us to reach our peak together. Never in my wildest dreams had I ever thought sex could feel like this. So completely and utterly consuming.

The world falls away and all I feel is Ren's breathing, his chest rising and falling to the rhythm of my heart.

My heart.

That's what this man is, and as sure as I know the sky is blue, not a day will go by where I let myself live without him.

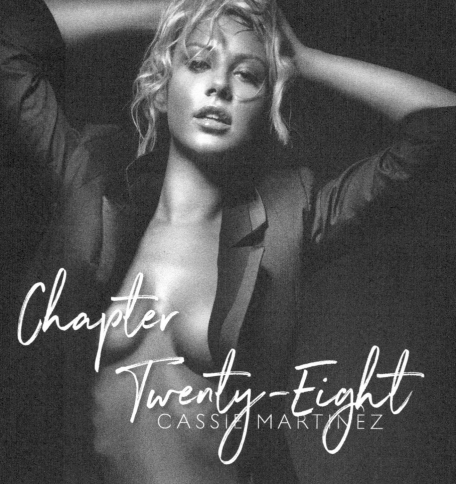

Chapter Twenty-Eight
CASSIE MARTINEZ

I T'S THE MORNING after *the* most amazing sex of my life. I know I've said that before, but I swear it just keeps getting better and better.

That paired with that earth-shattering connection we shared, and I feel as if I'm floating on a cloud.

Strolling into the kitchen, I pull open the sleek cabinet door and select a mug. For a bachelor, he sure does have quite the collection. The one I'm picking this morning has antlers à la National Lampoon Christmas Vacation.

I chuckle as I pour steaming black liquid into it. Ren is a

walking dichotomy. Here is this strong, intense, and highly domineering man; but dig a little deeper and you see that there's a kid inside who loves to play and just wants to be loved.

Last night he let me take control, showing me that I have nothing to fear when it comes to him. I couldn't possibly love that man more.

Speaking of the devil, his shirtless self walks in, positioning himself behind me and kissing me on the cheek.

"Morning, gorgeous. I don't think I could ever tire of seeing you in my home."

I gently nudge him in the ribs, playfully correcting him, "*Our* home."

He grins, squeezing me tight. "Yes, *our* home. Speaking of which, when are you wanting to clear out your loft? I can get some of my men together."

"I was thinking later today. Have you been able to figure out if there's a loophole in the contract I signed with the Wilson family?"

"Yes, our in-house team got back to me on Friday. He said it's difficult but doable. I also spoke to Ashely while we were up at the Cape and she said she'd be happy to set up a brunch where you could meet several of her friends, and your future clients."

My whole body hums with excitement. Everything is falling into place perfectly and I couldn't ask for a single thing more. For the first time in my life, I feel truly blessed.

"Ugh, I'm so ready to be done with that family. I just wish I could quit right this second, but it's the weekend and I have no idea where their latest social obligations have landed them."

"Well I have it on good authority that Woodrow is at his office right now, along with Barbie." He takes a sip of coffee from my mug, his eyes glittering with challenge.

"Should I be wondering how or why you know this?" I raise a brow and purse my lips—*slightly*. Let's not get carried away now, I'm not Blair.

"You don't want to know. But if you want to be rid of them as bad as you say you do, you should make it down there fairly quickly. Not sure how long they'll stick around and Blair is away at some plastic surgery retreat."

I nearly spit out my coffee. "What more could that woman have done? I'm pretty sure every square inch of her body is fake at this point."

I shake my head as I plant a kiss on my man's cheek, needing to stand on tiptoe in order to reach my target. "Thanks, babe. We can talk about the how and why of your knowledge later. I have a contract to break!"

Clapping my hands excitedly, I head to the bedroom. Though I wish I could walk out the door this second, it'd probably be a good idea if I put on something other than Ren's oversized hoodie.

Just as Ren had predicted, Wilson's flashy yellow hummer is parked in his spot. I make my way into the elevator and punch in the number to his floor. Freedom from the McCreepster, here I come!

The doors slide open and the marble-tiled hallway leads me to the glass doors where Dr. Woodrow Wilson, Board Certified Plastic

Surgeon, is etched. Hoping to make this the last time I step through them, I push with gusto, a massive smile splayed across my face.

Barbie looks up, surprised to see me. "Cassie, what a delight! What can I do you for?" Her bubbly personality seems dimmed today as if something's dulled her shine.

My smile turns downward. "Everything okay, hun?"

"Yup. Right as rain. Even better now that you're here. I'm guessing you came for our coffee date?"

Crap. How can I turn her down after that. *I can't.*

"Actually, I came to see the doc, but I'd love to grab some coffee on my way out. Is that cool?"

"Cool as a cucumber." She shoots me a blinding grin and I finally have the old Barbie back.

"Great! Is it okay if I head back? He's not with a patient, is he?"

"Nope, go right ahead. Our special client left right before you got in. Lucky you." She winks before looking down at her files once more.

"Thanks!" I'm practically squealing on my way to McCreeperson's office. Now that Dad is back at the house and Mom doesn't need my help, I'm free to hand this man his ass, and I truly couldn't be happier about it.

Ren

"What the fuck do you mean she's gone missing?!" I tighten my grip around the phone, making it creak under the pressure. "You're part of the top security team in the country and you can't even keep track of *one* woman?!"

"I'm sorry boss. She was there one moment and gone the next."

Un-fucking-believable. At least I know her last whereabouts was McCreeperson's office. No doubt he has her somewhere now. I just need to get to him before he hurts my little angel. There's no redemption for him. He's a dead man as far as I'm concerned.

I grab my keys and head down to the floor where my private garage is housed, pulling out the Hennessey Venom. Time is of the essence and every second counts.

I don't trust the worthless men who were tasked with watching Cass so it's up to me to scour the scene where she was last seen. I pray I find something that will lead me to her in time. Visions of a lifeless Cassie flash before me and my knees practically buckle.

No. Fuck that. I refuse to live in a world without her. It's just not going to happen.

Before I know it, I'm swerving around the parking garage attached to the doctor's building. Thanking God for this beast of a machine that brought me here in record time.

My men are lined up, firing squad style and I don't blame them. They should be scared. I step out of the car and head straight to them.

"Give me all of the information you have." I glare, letting them know they're in no way off the hook for such a royal screwup.

"We lost her when she went into the doctor's office. She never came out. When we went to check the parking spot reserved for the doctor and his nurse, they were both gone." The detail lead shifts on his feet as he delivers the information. "There's a freight elevator reserved for maintenance. We believe she was taken down without our having eyes on her and then driven away. We can't locate her through her cell. Apparently, it was left behind."

I pinch the bridge of my nose as he holds up Cassie's bag. They better pray she's unharmed or heads will roll.

"Her bag was located in the rear stairwell. We believe it was used to get to another floor and access the freight elevator from there."

"Have you combed through the doctor's office? There could be clues as to where he took her." I bore holes into the lead's head. He needs to be thankful I don't have laser vision like some sort of twisted superhero, or he'd be toast.

"We have men up there right now."

"Not good enough. Too damn slow." I move past him and head to the office myself. I guess the old adage is true, if you want anything done right, you need to do it yourself.

Busting through the glass doors, I head straight for the hallway that leads me to McCreeperson's office. I'm about to turn the corner when a scarf in Barbie's desk area catches my attention.

Wasn't Cassie wearing that in her hair this morning?

Tugging at the scarf, the drawer it's caught on pulls open. "*Well, fuck me.*"

A shrine. A fucking shrine. Dedicated to none other than Dr. McCreeperson. It seems Barbie is a little obsessed. There's even a badly photoshopped picture of her and the good doc included in the mix. It's clear to see that the body attached to Barbie's face is that of Blair, complete with chardonnay in hand.

I radio the men immediately, "Get every known address for Barbie, the doctor's nurse, and tap into every resource available. We need to get eyes on her ASAP. We find her and we'll find my Cass."

ACTS OF SALVATION

My stomach turns. This is somehow worse. At least the doctor held some affection toward my angel. But this psycho bitch is undoubtedly driven by nothing but hate and jealousy. There's no telling what she'll do.

Only one thing is certain, if she's hurt one hair on my baby's head, there will be hell to pay.

Chapter Twenty-Nine
CASSIE MARTINEZ

AN HOUR EARLIER...

I knock on Dr. McCreeperson's door, ready to get this show over with. There's no doubt that he'll try to pull some sort of theatrics.

He can get as pouty as he wants, but if he puts one of those grubby little hands on me, I won't hold back.

Mace in the face.

"Cassie, what a surprise. You've come to see me, and on a weekend where Blair is away." Woodrow smiles from ear to ear. "Have you thought over my proposal?"

ELEANOR ALDRICK

Simmer down, little man. Simmer down. This isn't what you think.

"Not sure what proposal you're talking about. What I do know is that I've come here to give you my resignation. As of this moment, I no longer work for you." I hand him a piece of paper Ren printed out for me. It outlines the grounds on which I'd be able to break the employment contract.

His hand shoots out, snatching the paper from me before tossing it onto his desk, not even sparing it a glance. "Come now, I'm sure we could come to some sort of agreement. Is it more money you want?"

My whole body shudders, "I'm not sure what women you're used to dealing with but I can't be bought with money." I turn to walk out but his hand shoots out once more, grabbing my wrist and yanking me toward him.

My body slams against his, his erection pressing into my thigh, and I just about vomit on his suit.

"Cassie, I'm more of a man than Ren will ever be. I can give you so much mo—" The disgusting asshole falls to the ground, clutching his eyes as if his life depended on it.

Mace in the face.

I tuck the bottle back into my bag as the doctor writhes in agony.

"No means no, Dr. McCreeperson. Let that be a lesson to you." Though there's no way his swollen eyes could see, I wave a finger in the air in a lecturing manner before turning to walk away.

"You'll pay for this!" he screeches from his position on the floor.

"If you come after me for self-defense, I'll let the world know

ACTS OF SALVATION

exactly why I quit. Try explaining *that* to the medical board." I resume my point of direction once more and walk away, leaving him in stunned silence. *Well, except for the noises of agony, that is.*

I'm strutting my way to the reception area when Barbie's overly eager grin stops me in my tracks. I was ready to walk out those doors, completely forgetting about my coffee date with her.

"You ready? I know just the cutest little cafe. It's down the street. They have a *chocolaterie* right inside, serving the most delicious bonbons with their coffee."

"Yes. That sounds amazing." I'm thinking of how I'm going to reward myself with a box of bonbons when Barbie's question has me stopping short of her desk.

"Oh, have you seen my puppy dog? He's the cutest thing you've ever seen."

"Can't say that I have. I didn't know you were a dog person! We'll have to introduce your baby to Bruce. I'm sure he'd love a playdate." I'm about to start walking again when her words stop me once more.

"Look, I keep a picture of him in here." She pulls open a drawer, and as my eyes land on its contents, I can't help but lean in closer.

Is that a shrine? Little clippings of fabric are attached to pictures of Barbie and Dr. Wilson, all clearly photoshopped.

A sharp prick on my neck has me whipping my head around in shock. Squinting my very heavy lids, I see Barbie with a grin, a very sick and sadistic grin. *What in the world?*

As the light dims around me, I send up a prayer, hoping someone finds me in time before this twisted nurse goes full Kevorkian.

ELEANOR ALDRICK

My head is pounding and my mouth is dry. I'm finally waking up from a horrible nightmare when I realize my hands and feet are bound with something plastic, cutting into my skin with every move I make.

It wasn't a dream. I've really been kidnapped by a psycho nurse. I'm about to open my eyes and attempt to roll onto my back when I hear Barbie's voice. She's talking to someone...pleading.

"I brought her here for *you*—so we could share. If you want her so badly, then I'm willing to split my time with her. I'd even be willing to sleep with her if it means you'll touch me again."

What in the hell?

"You've really gone and done it now, Barbie. First of all, I've told you time and time again that we're through. I'm done with your pussy." Dr. McCreeperson's voice, laden with disgust, bounces off the walls of the room. I can tell it's not large since the sound isn't traveling very far. Immediately my mind races, trying to figure out where I am. Thankfully, I don't have to wait long for an answer.

"Second of all, what in the hell makes you think drugging and kidnapping someone is okay? And to top it all off, you go and bring her to my home." I can hear the tinkling of a crystal decanter followed by the sound of a pour. "Sure, I'd like to fuck that hot piece of ass, but I'm not willing to lose my license over it."

My heart picks up at the realization of what those words mean. These two sick assholes have me at their mercy. Surely, he must know there's no way out of this without him getting into trouble.

And he clearly just said he doesn't think I'm worth the risk, so that leaves only one option...

"We have to get rid of her. Now, before she wakes up." Dr. Wilson's words suck all the air out of my lungs. "Barbie, get something to gag her. Can't risk her waking up on the way to the boat."

A second later, my mouth is being stuffed and covered with something that can be tied around my head.

"Done," Barbie's not so cheery voice declares.

A set of hands pick me up, throwing me over narrow shoulders. It must be Woodrow. There's no way Barbie could lift me like this. I lay limply trying to give the illusion of being knocked out cold, when in reality I'm trying to figure out how I'm going to get out of this mess.

Through narrowed slits, I see we've entered the garage. Quite possibly the largest garage I've ever seen. It even puts Ren's car collection to shame.

My god. Are all of his cars yellow?

Barbie turns, and I quickly shut my eyes. If I were alone with just one of them, I could attempt some of the moves I've learned in Krav Maga, but with it being two of them I need to decide if my taking offensive action is worth exposing the fact that I'm awake.

"Open the trunk. We're taking the sedan." The detached tone in Woodrow's voice sends chills up my spine. It's almost as if he's done this before.

Whatever blood had rushed to my head has now completely drained. It's at least a hundred degrees outside and summers in Texas are extremely brutal.

Putting me in the trunk is a death sentence. There's no way I'll survive.

With a thud, I land on top of a spare tire and let out a muffled grunt. It takes everything in me not to cry out in pain.

Unconscious people don't yelp, do they?

The slamming of the trunk has me opening my eyes and trying to adjust to the non-existent light of the confined area. Most modern cars come equipped with safety latches in the cargo, but given the fact that I'm completely bound and in the dark, searching for one is extremely difficult.

I'm wiggling my body like a worm, trying to touch my face to whatever solid surface I can reach. Maybe, just maybe, if I'm able to locate the latch with my face, I can somehow get it to open for me.

Nothing. I can't feel a damn thing other than the smooth lining of the trunk.

I'm about to go searching for the damn latch again when we hit a bump in the road, sending my body flying and slamming against the roof of the trunk.

As I land back on the floor, my head hits something hard and sharp. I wince, trying to suppress a yell. To my horror, something thick and wet touches my cheek. The metallic scent of the liquid tells me it's probably blood. *My blood.*

Voices from the cab pull my attention. *Maybe they're stopping?* A girl can hope.

"It's pretty hot out. Is she going to be okay back there?" Barbie's voice cracks with her question. Could the psychopath have a conscience?

"Probably not." There's a long pause. "Don't look at me like that. You're the one who brought her to me. I'm simply cleaning up the mess you've made."

ACTS OF SALVATION

Another bump in the road sends my head careening against the metal of the trunk, making my head feel as if it's going to cave in.

The combination of the drugs, heat, and trauma… I'm not sure I can hold out much longer.

Sweat drips into my eyes—*Or is that blood?*—as the voices in the cab become muffled.

It's hard to make out what they're saying now. My head is pounding and my ears are ringing as everything becomes fuzzy.

Air. I need air.

With each inhalation, my lungs catch fire and no matter how hard I try, I can't breathe.

A voice inside me whispers. *It's time to let go.*

Closing my eyes to the darkness, I say one last prayer and thank God for all the good I've received in my life.

In my short nineteen years, I've managed to experience true love, which is more than most could say.

Too bad I won't live to enjoy it.

Chapter Thirty
REN MORETTI

"WE'VE GOT EYES on her," Titus' voice booms through the car speaker.

"Send me the location. I'm on my way now."

"She's moving. The doctor and nurse are heading west on I-30." There's a pause and I can tell Titus is holding back.

"Spit it out, brother."

"We think she's in the trunk. There are no visuals of her in the car, which means she's either in the trunk or…"

Fuck. I don't even want to think of the alternative. It's already bad enough she might be in the trunk. Shifting gears, I head west.

who could stop them? Have you reached out to our connections with the local PD?"

"Right now, all we have is aerial confirmation, but Hudson is on the phone with the police to intercept. She's nearing Cockerel Hill now."

Thank god. She isn't far. Pressing on the accelerator, I push this car to its limit. "I need to get to her before it's too late. Did you send me their location?"

"Done, brother. Their coordinates should be on your nav now."

"Thank you," I choke out as I cut the line. Checking the upgraded system attached to the central control panel, I hit accept on the new coordinates. "Hang on, baby. I'm coming."

I see it. The silver of the Mercedes sedan gleams in the hot midday sun, pulling me toward it like a beacon.

My mind races as I gain on the doctor's car. Not giving a shit about safety, I swing my Venom in front of them, downshifting almost immediately.

Objective attained. They hit their brakes, slowing down their vehicle to a slow roll. Just as I'm about to park my sports car in the middle of a four-lane highway, a full police guard flanks either side of the Mercedes, with one getting directly between me and the doctor.

Good. They can deal with the shitbags while I go for Cass.

Exiting the vehicle, I start to round one of the squad cars when I hear my name being called.

"Ren." The voice stops me in my tracks. "Hang back. We've got this."

Quickly glancing to my right without lowering my gun, I see the young sergeant and recognize him instantly. WRATH Securities helped him break the case that landed him his current position with the police department.

"Marcus, with all due respect, these sick bastards have my girl in the trunk. You'll have to pump me full of bullets before I let anyone get in the way of her rescue."

He nods, reluctantly letting me take the lead as I move forward.

I hear him tell his men to stand down until further instruction, giving me the opening to head straight for the driver's side of the sedan.

My gun's out and ready to play if the asshole behind the wheel gets any ideas. Through the windshield, I see Dr. Wilson's eyes widen in horror. *That's right buddy, I'm coming for you.*

"Open the fucking door and I won't shoot you." *Yet.* Regardless of whatever this guy does from this point forward, his ass is mine.

Dr. Wilson's hands slowly come up, palm facing toward me in a supplicating gesture. "Okay, okay. No need to shoot."

Barbie squeaks from behind him. "We were just heading to Eagle Mountain Lake for some summer fun. Is there a crime against boating on a hot day?"

"*Shut. Up,*" Dr. Wilson spits out through gritted teeth, each word coming out in staccato.

My blood boils. They were going to dump her body. That's it.

There's not a soul on this earth that could save them from my wrath.

I grab Dr. Wilson by the shirt and slam him into the ground. Watching as his face bounces off the hot asphalt, I pin him down with the underside of my boot while popping the trunk release with my right hand. "Can someone take this sick bastard?"

An officer quickly takes him off my hands, giving me the opening I needed to get Cass. I round the car and look into the trunk. What I see shatters my already jagged heart.

Cass laying in a pool of blood, her body limp and unconscious. Lifting her body, I bring her to my chest and carry her bridal style to the ground. "I've got you, baby. I've got you."

I smooth away the matted and bloody hair from her face. *God, how did I let this happen?* "Please don't leave me, little angel. I need you. You're my light in this dark world."

Afraid of what I'll find, I finally press a finger to her pulse. *Nothing.* I get nothing.

"*Fuuuuuuuck!*" I roar into the wind, not giving a shit about my surroundings. Tears I haven't shed in over a decade fall unbidden as I rock her against my chest, clinging to her body with every bit of strength I possess.

My fucking angel, my love. I let her down and now she's gone. She's left me.

"Ren," a whisper of a voice brings my attention downward. *Could it be?*

Cass's eyes are still closed but I swear I see her lips move. "Where the fuck is the EMT, we need a medical kit, now!" I bark out, unwilling to rip my eyes away from her for even a second.

Someone comes from behind me, a stretcher not far behind. Lifting her up, I place her body onto the raised surface as they take her vitals.

"We've got a heartbeat! It's faint, but it's there!" A scrawny guy in his early twenties beams and I swear I just about kiss him.

They start a drip and begin to wheel her into an ambulance, but before she's hoisted into it, she calls out my name once more, "Ren."

"Shhh. I'm right here, baby." I'm glad she's speaking but I want her to conserve as much energy as possible. I'm about to tell her to stop talking when her next words absolutely gut me. "Your mom. She's beautiful, just like you."

My eyes prickle with the promise of more tears, "*My mom?*"

"Yes, she brought me back to you." Cassie's gaze falls behind me. On instinct, I turn, but of course there's nothing there. Her eyes shutter closed as she utters her next words. "Mhm. She loves her little sugar bug."

My heart practically stops in my chest, goose bumps covering every square inch of my body. *What in the actual fuck? There's no way she could possibly know.*

I was born with a visible vein across the bridge of my nose, which I eventually grew out of. But its non-technical term is a sugar bug, and it also happened to be my mother's term of endearment for me.

The fact that she chose to use that term right now has me stuttering for air.

"Are you getting in or will you be following?" The young paramedic pulls me out of my thoughts as he lifts Cassie into the emergency vehicle.

"You bet your ass I'm coming. I don't think anything could pull me away from this woman's side." Hopping into the ambulance, I pull my phone out and shoot the guys a group text.

REN: The Venom is on I-30. Need someone to take it home for me.

HUDSON: Dibs! I'm about five minutes out.

TITUS: What do you want to do with the kidnappers? Local PD are holding them back for us for further instruction. I told them you might want access before proper booking.

REN: Please intercept and take them to our friends in New York, the Renzetti's.

God, I love my job. It's allowed us to make connections I would've never thought possible. One of them being the Renzetti *Famiglia* who currently owe us a favor for facilitating a rescue on their behalf.

Thankfully, Titus picks up on what I'm saying without my having to put anything else in writing.

TITUS: Ten-Four, Brother. Keep us posted on Cassie's status.

REN: Will do, and thank you for all of your help today. I appreciate it.

I'll deal with Cassie's kidnappers once she's doing better. There's no way in hell I'm leaving her side while she's in this state. In the meantime, I'm fully confident the Renzetti's can keep them

ACTS OF SALVATION

occupied until it's time to dole out their justice.

Cassie

The incessant beeping of an alarm clock has me waking up from the strangest dream. I was floating on a cloud with the prettiest angel. Her long blond hair looked to be spun of gold, and the scent of baked goods and flowers followed her wherever she'd go.

"Can someone turn off that damn alarm?" I groan, needing that infernal racket to stop.

A chorus of gasps and chuckles has my eyes cracking open, but barely. I see that I'm in a hospital room, flooded with flowers and balloons. *Damn, how long have I been here?*

Ren is sitting to my left, looking completely a mess. Hair disheveled with the onset of a decent beard starting to appear. In front of me, my mom, sisters, and Bella approach the bed—grins splayed across their tired faces.

"Mija, you're awake!" My mother wipes away at her tears while Ren squeezes my hand.

"I've gone ahead and buzzed the nurse," His voice comes out choked as if trying to hold back emotion. Visions of him bent over me in an open highway flash before my eyes. They're aerial views as if I were floating above him.

Slowly but surely, everything starts coming back to me.

"Oh my god. The doctor... Barbie..." My body tenses at the memory, the monitors clearly picking up on the increase of my heartbeat.

"Shhhhh, Cass. You're safe now." Ren gently strokes my arm as my heart resumes its regular rhythm. "It's all been handled." The certainty in his voice brings me comfort, letting me relax back into the bed. I'll need more information on that later but for now, his word is all I need.

"Did someone push the call button?" An older gentleman in a white coat walks into the room trailed by a nurse in blue scrubs. "Oh, Miss Martinez. I see that you're up! I was about to do rounds when one of the nurses informed me there was a notification coming from your room."

"Yes..." the one word comes out slow and full of apprehension. Narrowing my eyes into thin slits, I judge the man's words with the scrutiny of a Bible thumpin' preacher. I mean, you can't really blame me for being overly cautious after my last run-in with a doctor and his nurse.

"Great. When you arrived at the hospital, you'd suffered a pretty significant laceration to the back of your head, lost a lot of blood, and were severely dehydrated. Needless to say, you were in pretty rough shape."

"How long ago was that?" My mind spins with all of this information.

"A little over twenty-four hours. It's a good sign that you're awake and coherent now, though. We'll be running some tests and—barring any red flags—you should be cleared to go home as early as tonight."

Ren squeezes my hand, a glance over to him letting me see his gorgeous smile and that sexy dimple of his. *I'm so ready to be home with this man.*

ACTS OF SALVATION

Looking back toward the doctor, I give him my biggest and brightest smile, "Okay, let's get this party started. I'm ready to blow this popsicle stand."

As soon as the doctor and his nurse exit the room, the questions start flying.

"Soooo, are either of you going to tell me what's going on between the two of you?" Bella's smirk lets me know there's no sense in denying the obvious.

Ren's been clinging to my hand as if his life depended on it. I think it's pretty clear he has some sort of sentimental attachment to me.

Without warning, a dull throb begins at the base of my neck, sending my hands up to my head in a futile attempt to make the discomfort stop.

"*Bella!*" Ren barks. "Now is not the time for playing twenty questions."

"It's fine. I'm fine." I try to smooth the tension between my best friend and her uncle.

"You're not. As much as it pains me to admit this, Uncle Ren is right." Bella gives me a sad smile. "I'm so sorry you're going through all of this, but as soon as you're back home, I'm coming over and we're having one of our famous nights in."

"Heads-up, we're inviting ourselves," Aria chimes in on behalf of herself and Carmen.

I softly chuckle, letting my head softly fall back on the pillow. Looking to my right, I see my mother's eyes glistening with freshly shed tears. She's been quiet this entire time, *very* unlike her.

"Ma, you okay?" My brows press together as I wait for an answer.

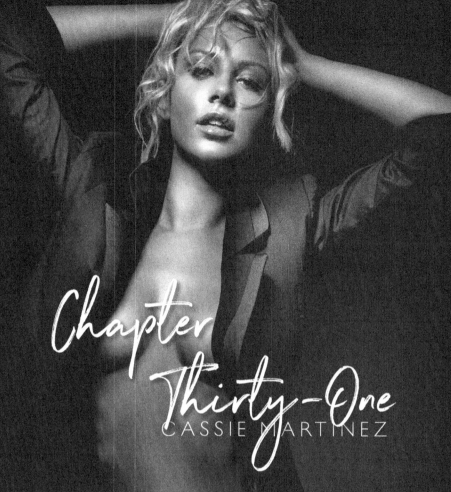

Chapter Thirty-One
CASSIE MARTINEZ

"THANK YOU FOR STAYING by my side while I was at the hospital. Mom told me you didn't even leave to go shower." My thumb strokes the top of Ren's hand as he drives us home.

"Of course. There's nowhere else I'd rather be, even with my niece grilling me about the two of us and what we have. Let me tell you, there's no sidestepping a subject with her. It's a miracle I got her to drop it while you recover." Ren blows out a breath, remembering Bella's interrogation tactics.

"Are you wanting to keep us a secret a little longer?" My heart can't help but deflate a little at the idea of his not wanting us to be public.

"Are you crazy? I love you and now that you've admitted to loving me back, there's nowhere to move but forward."

"Don't say that around my mom. She's bound to break out her little black book and start making plans." I chuckle to myself, remembering how my mom reacted when first meeting Ren.

Ren laughs but his heart isn't in it. *Poor guy.* I must've traumatized him with my rejection of his proposal.

Squeezing his hand, I turn my gaze toward the window but my brows furrow as I take in our surroundings. "Where are we going?"

We're in Ren's G-Wagon but instead of heading toward downtown, Ren exits the highway, taking us down a path toward White Rock Lake.

"To get a do-over." His tone is clipped but playful.

"What?" I laugh, unsure of what he's talking about.

"You'll see." He winks while biting at the edge of his bottom lip.

We get on a road that winds around the massive lake where

sailboats and kayakers drift by. It's a gorgeous day, and the sun that had previously been my demise is now warming the multiple parkgoers as they go about their daily activities.

My curiosity is growing to an all-time high when Ren suddenly pulls into a hidden driveway. *What in the world?*

The SUV slowly drives up a winding path and behind the beautiful tree-lined drive stands a modern ranch style home.

Its stunning all-white brick facade is contrasted with black trimming and a black metal roof. Massive windows span the entire front of the home, no doubt put in to take advantage of the views.

Sure enough, stepping out of the car you're able to look back toward the park and get a full view of the lake.

"What are we doing here?" Looking toward Ren, I see that he's exchanged his smile for a nervous smirk.

"We're home."

"What?" I'm pretty sure I suffered a concussion along with all the other stuff I had going on because there's no way this is real life.

"I'd put an offer in on this place when we were on our way back from the Cape. They accepted and I had them sign over a temporary lease until closing. That way we could have full access while the paperwork is completed."

"But why?" I see that my words raise a little panic in my gorgeous man's face, so I wrap my arms around his torso in order to soothe him. "Babe, I love it. I'm just wondering what on earth possessed you to do this?"

"Security. While we were at the hospital, the team came by and wired the entire place, setting up a new security system that will keep our family safe. It's a hell of a lot safer than you would be in some high-rise."

His use of the word 'family' has warmth blooming in my chest. The idea of Ren running around chasing our babies in this yard has my ovaries practically bursting with excitement.

"Do you like it?"

"No, I don't like it. I love it!" I shake my head at him in disbelief. "You'd have to be a crazy person not to."

His face lights up and I can tell he feels proud of his decision. Though I wish he would have included me in the process of finding our new home, I know how important safety and security are to him, so I'm willing to let it slide.

Looking around the grounds, I can't help but grin. "This is exactly what I envisioned my dream home would look like. It's as if you dove into my mind and plucked it straight from my imagination."

"Close. I may or may not have peeked at your Pinterest board. But in my defense, you'd left the browser open." Ren dons a smile as he squeezes me tighter. "But hey, you can't be mad with a view like this, right?"

He motions toward the lake, making me take in another view of our new reality. Just as I'm about to look back at him I see four sailboats with black writing on their mainsails.

My knees buckle and my eyes water as I read what they say.

WILL. YOU. MARRY. ME?

Turning back toward Ren, I see that he's down on one knee holding a gorgeous solitaire diamond on a thin platinum band.

"Cassandra Marie Martinez, my little angel. When I was at my darkest, you saved me. When I thought life wasn't worth living, you brought me hope. When I'd lost my way and forgotten the meaning of life, you showed me the way. Let me spend the rest of my life showing you my gratitude and unconditional love... will you do me the honor of becoming my partner in life—my other half?"

"Yes! A million times, yes!" I fling myself toward him, enveloping him in my arms. "I love you so much, Ren." I tackle him to the ground and ferociously attack his mouth.

Someone whistling has me reluctantly pulling away from Ren. Looking up, I see that it's coming from Bella, who's standing by the front double doors to the home.

"I love you like a sister and I'm happy you'll officially be a part of the family, but I'm not exactly ready to see you making out with my uncle." Bella grins while rushing toward us.

The whole gang exits through the front doors, and Ren even managed to con my mom and sisters into showing up without spoiling the surprise. A massive feat since my sisters don't know the meaning of a secret.

Before I can get a word out, I'm surrounded by my loved ones, being smothered in congratulatory kisses and hugs.

I'm so damn happy.

Looking at Ren, I say, "This is one hell of a do-over, babe."

Bella tugs at my arm, pulling my attention back to her, "Hold up, Ren's proposed to you more than once? You have some serious filling in to do missy. Don't think you're off the hook from keeping all of this from me."

I place my hand on her belly while raising a brow, "Looks like I wasn't the only one keeping secrets. How about we go inside and catch up on everything?"

As I'm pulling my best friend into our new home, Ren bellows from behind, "Not *everything*. She's still my niece!"

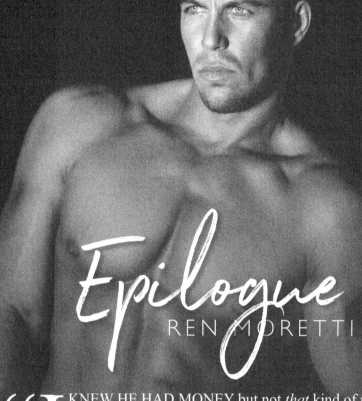

Epilogue
REN MORETTI

"I KNEW HE HAD MONEY but not *that* kind of money," Cassie's sister, Aria, not so quietly whispers to my fiancée as she strokes the leather seat she's in.

I silently laugh to myself. We're in our private jet and not too long ago, Cassie was in that very seat doing the same exact thing.

I let out a sigh of contentment. There is no greater pleasure than knowing I'm able to provide my little angel with experiences beyond her wildest dreams, and by extension, her family too.

If anyone deserves life's riches, it's most definitely her. On more than one occasion, her acts have been my salvation. I don't think I could ever fully repay her for what she's given me—but I sure as fuck am gonna try.

"Aria, you know he can hear you right? He's sitting not ten feet away." Cassie rolls her eyes in irritation. Something I've noticed the sisters do a lot around each other. Regardless of their banter, those four are as thick as thieves. Even their sister Ceci gets in on the action from half a world away.

"Before we land, I wanted to let you know exactly what we'll be walking into." I suppress a smile with a twitch of my lip. "The Renzettis and the men of WRATH have a pact. *An understanding.* We've helped each other on countless occasions and I don't see that ending anytime soon."

Aria's eyes are wide, but not with fear. *No*, her eyes hold intrigue and hunger.

Interesting.

"Right. I remember meeting Johnny and Twitch when they were down in Texas for Silver's rescue. God, what those assholes put Silver through was sick." Cassie's beautiful mouth twists into a sneer.

"Don't worry. Everyone responsible got what they deserved," I assure them both, silently letting them know that where this family is concerned, justice will always be served.

"Well don't worry about me. I don't scare easy." Aria purses her lips, her eyes emitting a defiant glint.

"I wasn't worried. You're Cassie's sister, after all. She's a warrior." My hand reaches out to trace the contours of my angel's lips. I'll never tire of the gentle slopes and angles that make up her beautiful face.

"Stop looking at me like that or we're going to have to make use of the bedroom back there." Cassie's head motions toward the secret panel leading to the plane's private quarters.

"Holy fuck! There's a bedroom in here?!" Aria's comic look of surprise has all of us bursting out into a round of laughter, bringing a much-needed lightness to the air—and we definitely need light, given the darkness were about to encounter up ahead.

"Men, good to see you." One of my hands reaches out, grasping Gavriel Renzetti's forearm as I lean forward and clap his back with the other.

Motioning toward the women, I move forward with introductions. "This is my fiancée, Cassie, and her sister Aria."

Johnny DeLucci is the first to speak, "Cassie, it's good to see you again." He's greeting my fiancée but his eyes have yet to pry themselves from Aria. I swear if he looks at her any longer, her clothes are bound to burn off from the intensity.

"You've come to collect your trophies, I take it." Gavriel cuts into the awkward tension, for which I'm grateful.

Aria is a grown-ass woman, and I for one will not be cock blocking unless I know the douchebag in question is unworthy. But despite all that, I still would rather avoid it altogether.

"Yes. But I'd like a minute with them alone before transport."

"No problem." Gavriel holds open a door that leads to the exterior. "Ladies, if you'll follow me. I think it's time you met Sia. If what I hear about you is true, she'll want to talk your ear off all night."

He must be talking about Aria. She's a pretty amazing lyricist and has worked with some high-profile artists in the past. *Good.* I don't exactly want them around for what I have to do next.

Nodding toward them, I signal that it's okay to leave. Not because I control them, but because they know I'd never put them in harm's way. Trust is something I've had to earn with Cassie, and now that I have it, I'd be a damn fool to fuck it up.

As soon as they clear out, Johnny leads me back to a small room with no windows where two treacherous bodies lie on the ground—bound and gagged just as they'd done to my Cassie.

I feel no pity for these two. They've made their bed and now they're going to lay in it.

"Wakey wakey, eggs and bakey." I kick at Woodrow's body, needing him to be wide awake for what's about to go down.

I'm not a particularly violent man, though I'm more than capable should the occasion arise. *No.* My form of vengeance comes in a much different package. Silent and unassuming. To the outsider looking in, they'd be none the wiser.

And though I'd love to see this man writhing in physical pain, the blow I'm about to deliver is sure to be a million times worse.

Woodrow groans into his gag while his eyes crack open, letting me know he's awake and listening.

"You've been a very busy man, *doctor.*" That last word is spat out as if it were pure vile. "In my hand, I hold dozens of statements from previous patients of yours—all claiming sexual assault. Some of them were even minors." As if I didn't hate this man enough, the more I dug through his past, the more it revealed just what a sick bastard he really is.

He mumbles something unintelligible into his gag.

"Nah, ah, ahhhh." I wave a finger back and forth. "I'm not done yet." I hold up a piece of paper and bring it close to his face. "This right here proves that not only are you guilty of being a sexually sadistic bastard, but also an avid accomplice to insider trading. All those 'lucky' investments that helped make you your millions? All illegitimate. Highly Illegal."

The bastard has the audacity to cry. His eyes leak as a pathetic whimper escapes his mouth.

"Oh, but I'm not done. All of this has been turned into the authorities. And guess what? There's a warrant out for your arrest." I don the biggest grin since Cassie agreed to be my wife. "Lucky for you, I'm also a bounty hunter when need be, and word on the street is you and your accomplice here are fetching a pretty penny."

Barbie squirms in her restraints as a sequence of squeals escape her. One look at her and her bug eyes let me know she's been listening to every word I've said.

"Oh, yes, sweetheart. Don't think that we're leaving you unscathed. Everything pointed to you covering the doctor's tracks as far as his illicit groping sessions were concerned. Not to mention, there are several images of you with Woodrow here as he retrieved very sensitive information leading him to his investments." My wide grin turns into a maniacal one. "You, my dear Barbie, are also named on a warrant."

Barbie burst into full-blown hysterical wails, flailing herself against the wall in a futile attempt at escaping.

"Shhhh, Barbie. It's best you save your energy for prison. I hear they don't take too kindly to those who aid pedophiles." I turn my back to them, unable to look at their repulsive faces any longer.

Scum of the earth, that's what they are. But death would be too quick of a punishment. No, they deserved a slow tortured existence.

Nodding to Johnny, we exit the room, the guards resuming their post. With business handled, it's time for some fun.

I'm ready to show my angel why this is the city that never sleeps. Lucky for me, what I have in mind has nothing to do with the nightlife and everything to do with our bedroom.

Other Books

MEN OF WRATH SERIES (forbidden love):

ACTS OF ATONEMENT
age-gap/nanny/single dad

ACTS OF REDEMPTION
sister's ex/former Navy SEAL

ACTS OF GRACE
Brother's best friend

ACTS OF MERCY
age-gap/stepbrother

MAFIA ROMANCE:

OMERTA: A VERY MAFIOSO CHRISTMAS
Mozzafiato, prequel to MAGARI

MAGARI
Capo dei capi falls for an outsider

Let's stay connected. I'd love to hear what you thought of the book, what's on your TBR list, or simply how your day is going.

www.EleanorAldrick.com

Instagram
@EleanorAldrick

Goodreads
www.Goodreads.com/EleanorAldrick

Twitter
www.Twitter.com/EleanorAldrick

Facebook
www.Facebook.com/EleanorAldrick

Acknowledgments

Nope. I'm not Wonder Woman.

I'd like to say that I can do it all, but alas, I cannot.

The book you've just read could not have been created without the love and support of many.

First and foremost, my husband. The real MVP, who always encourages me and never complains about my late night, early morning, or all-nighter writing sprints. I love you to the moon and back.

My mother, who always taught me the value of hard work and perseverance. I would not be the woman I am today without you. You are forever in my heart.

My girl tribe, Domino, Taralyn, Natalie, Kellie, Ivette, Julie and Tracy. Thank you for always being so supportive, cheering me on and helping me thrive. I love you and I'm so glad you aren't sick of me and my stories yet.

My street team, the Sinfully Seductive Squad and all of the amazing bookstagrammers. Thank you for all that you do. Y'all are social media wizards!

And of course, you. Thank you. Thank you for taking the time to read my book. It honestly means the world to me. I hope that we can continue this journey together.

XoXo,
Eleanor Aldrick

Made in the USA
Monee, IL
03 March 2023

29085441R00149